Jimmy Coates is dead.
If NJ7 find out he isn't,
they're going to kill him.

Also by Joe Craig

1. *Jimmy Coates: Killer*

2. *Jimmy Coates: Target*

3. *Jimmy Coates: Revenge*

JOE CRAIG

HarperCollins *Children's Books*

First published in Great Britain by
HarperCollins *Children's Books* 2007
HarperCollins *Children's Books* is a
division of HarperCollins *Publishers* Ltd
77-85 Fulham Palace Road,
Hammersmith, London, W6 8JB

www.harpercollinschildrensbooks.co.uk

1

Copyright © Joseph Craig 2007

ISBN 13: 978 0 00 723286 4
ISBN 10: 0 00 723286 1

Joseph Craig asserts the moral right to be
identified as the author of the work.

Printed and bound in Great Britain by
Clays Ltd, St Ives plc

Mixed Sources
Product group from well-managed
forests and other controlled sources
www.fsc.org Cert no. SW-COC-1806
© 1996 Forest Stewardship Council

FSC is a non-profit international organisation established to promote the
responsible management of the world's forests. Products carrying the FSC
label are independently certified to assure consumers that they come
from forests that are managed to meet the social, economic and
ecological needs of present and future generations.

Find out more about HarperCollins and the environment at
www.harpercollins.co.uk/green

About the author

Joe Craig studied Philosophy at Cambridge University, then became a songwriter. Within a year, however, his love of stories had taken over and he was writing the first novel in the *Jimmy Coates* series. It was published in 2005. He is now a full-time author and likes to keep in touch with his readers through his website www.joecraig.co.uk.

When he's not writing he's visiting schools, playing the piano, inventing snacks, playing football, coaching cricket, reading or watching a movie.

He lives in London.

EIGHT YEARS PREVIOUSLY...

Twelve black dots crept through the night sky. They were only visible because the North Sea was relatively calm that night and the lights of the oil rig reflected off the water. In the wind, the night manager's tie blustered round his beard. He pulled his suit jacket tighter, but it was too small to cross over the front of his considerable stomach.

"Are they...?" he gasped. His words were lost beneath the constant pounding of the rig's machinery.

"I think they're helicopters, sir!" shouted a burly man next to him. "Do you know anything about this?"

The night manager shook his head and just caught his hard hat before it slipped off. He couldn't tear his eyes away from the horizon and the twelve silhouettes, moving like a pack of airborne panthers through the clouds. His mouth gaped in horror.

"Pack your belongings!" he yelled. "Tell everyone!"

"What?"

"They're coming here! Don't you see?" The night manager grabbed his colleague by the collar of his fluorescent work jacket. "I thought we'd be safe. I didn't believe they would actually ever do it! But they're coming!"

With that, he turned and ran as hard as he could back to his office, panting heavily. By the time he reached the office door, twelve helicopters were hovering over the rig. Their drone was as powerful as the thrashing noise of the rig. The night manager watched, a crunching panic in his heart.

From each chopper dropped twelve ropes, making the sky a grid of black lines. Then down each rope slid a black figure. The curve of each man's back was interrupted by the solid horizontal line of his machine gun. The night manager collapsed against his office door.

Seconds later, a giant man loomed over him. He hitched his machine gun behind his back, pulled off his balaclava and held out a hand. His face looked like a veil of skin had been stretched over a construction of iron scaffolding.

"Get up!" he ordered. "I'm the commanding officer of this SAS unit. This oil rig is now the property of the British Government and temporarily under my supervision. Instruct your staff that you will all be leaving at 07:00, when a new workforce will arrive to take over."

At last the night manager gathered the strength to slap the soldier's hand away.

"You can't do this!" he screamed. "This rig is owned by a private company! You're stealing it!"

"I'm nationalising it."

"Is that what the Government calls stealing now?"

The soldier dug his heel into the night manager's beard and pushed him all the way to the floor. "So call the police," he grunted.

He stepped over the night manager into the office, looking down his nose at the shelves of exotic ornaments that had obviously been collected from all over the world. He ran his finger along the edge of a checked board, covered in an arrangement of shiny black and white stones.

"Don't touch that!" the night manager pleaded, sitting up against the door. "Please! I'm in the middle of a game."

"A game? Looks like a bunch of stones to me."

"Yes, yes, but it's a Padukp'an board. An ancient Chinese game."

"Paduk-what?"

"Padukp'an." The night manager was panting even harder now and constantly wiping sweat from his face. The soldier thought for a moment, then announced,

"I like this. I'm keeping it."

"What?" the night manager squealed. "You can't! It's mine!"

The soldier took a seat behind the desk. "The rig is

the British Government's," he declared, "and that game is now mine."

"But you don't even know how to play!"

"I'll teach myself," said the SAS man. "Now get out of my office."

01 *EXILE*

When you know the British Secret Service wants you dead, it's hard to relax. But Jimmy Coates was forcing himself to try. Every second that passed, every mile he was driven away from New York, it became a tiny bit easier. No hand burst through the window of the car to grab him. No sirens pierced the quiet drone of the road. He had really done it. He had fooled NJ7, the top-secret British intelligence agency. They thought he was dead.

According to NJ7 files, Jimmy Coates – the boy their scientists had genetically designed to grow into a killer – had been terminated by machine-gun fire and his body lost in New York's East River. They could call off the search. Jimmy didn't want to let himself smile. Not yet. He wasn't far enough away.

"Welcome to Blackfoot Airbase," announced Agent Froy, the CIA man who had grasped Jimmy by the shoulder to lift him out of the East River a few hours before.

The black sedan slowed down and Froy pulled into a driveway. The iron gate in front of them rolled back automatically. Jimmy sat up in his seat to look for whatever device must have identified the car. His eyes scanned the foliage that lined the road. The hedge wasn't a hedge; he noticed that immediately. It was an iron wall, six metres high and at least a metre thick, constructed to resemble a line of Leyland cypress trees and painted dark green.

In a second, Jimmy picked out four security cameras and a laser scanner all concealed in the fake hedge. A cockroach couldn't get into this place without being microwaved by the lasers first.

He twisted in his seat as they drove through and watched the gate slide back into place. The last sliver of the rest of the world disappeared. He was cut off from everything, sealed inside Blackfoot, the classified military airbase on the outskirts of Piscataway, New Jersey.

Jimmy's family was a lifetime away. He had left his sister Georgie and his best friend Felix Muzbeke with Felix's parents back in New York. They were also in the care of the CIA. Jimmy could see them now, in the safehouse apartment above a Korean restaurant in Chinatown. He didn't know when the CIA would relocate them, but he hoped it would be soon.

Meanwhile, his mother had been on her way to find

Christopher Viggo, the former NJ7 agent who had helped Jimmy escape Britain. Viggo had run off back to Britain, full of anger. Jimmy pictured him trying to overthrow the Government single-handed.

He had to hold on to the hope that he would see them all again. Even if it wasn't for several years, whatever happened or however he changed, Jimmy knew he must always remember his family.

But Jimmy had no idea how he would change. Inside him was a powerful organic programming. It enabled him to do amazing things, but day by day the assassin instincts in his DNA took over more of his mind, subduing his human voice. Would that voice become just an echo in his memory? And what if his memory itself was pushed aside to make room for the assassin's skill?

For a horrible minute, Jimmy imagined himself in a few years' time, about to turn eighteen. His programming would be fully developed – what would he feel when he looked at a picture of his mum? Or Georgie? Would they be like forgotten files, lost in the back of a computer's hard-drive, never accessed? Jimmy tried to imagine looking without any hint of emotion, thinking of them as just two more faces. It made him feel sick, so he closed his eyes and dropped his head back on to the leather.

A few seconds later, the car stopped abruptly.

Jimmy sat up. The long driveway had opened out to reveal an expanse of concrete stretching for at least two miles ahead of them. Right in the middle was a one-storey breeze-block bunker, covered in a jumble of satellite dishes.

The wind whipped across the tarmac, buffeting the side of the car. There was none of the noise or bustle found at a commercial airport. The place was deserted.

"Where are the planes?" Jimmy asked.

Froy was busy punching numbers into his mobile phone. "That's what I'm going to find out," he grumbled. Then he barked into his phone, "Where's our plane?!"

Jimmy leaned forwards, but he couldn't make out what the person on the end of the line was saying.

"Get one down here now! Anyone!" Froy went on. "I don't care about the weather conditions. Colonel Keays is overseeing this operation himself. There are only two people more powerful than Colonel Keays: the President and God Almighty. Have either of them called you? No. So get the closest military air vehicle out of the sky and on to that runway."

Froy snapped his phone shut and stuffed it back into his pocket. "Sorry, Jimmy. An operation like this is usually planned weeks in advance. This obviously had to be a bit last-minute."

Jimmy felt the panic swirling in his chest. He had to

get as far away from NJ7 as possible, as quickly as possible. Every second he spent sitting in the back of that car was a second too long.

"Don't worry," Froy reassured him. "Your plane was diverted to McGuire because of high winds, but I'm not going to let a little breeze get in our way. I've told them to ignore the weather. They'll find us something."

How long will that take? Jimmy wondered – though he didn't dare say it aloud. He scanned the sky. With nothing to distract him, he couldn't help returning to one thought he wanted more than anything to forget about for now – his father. It still seemed amazing to Jimmy, but Ian Coates had just taken over as Prime Minister of Great Britain.

Already the man had shown that he planned to continue the policy of not letting the public vote. He called it 'Neo-democracy' and the more Jimmy found out about it, the worse it sounded. The Government held on to absolute control, with no opposition, and everything was run by the Secret Service.

Even worse than that, Ian Coates had threatened to go to war with France over a tiny misunderstanding. The only thing that had stopped him so far was the fact that the American President wasn't going to support him unless Britain spent billions of dollars on American weapons.

In spite of all this, the one thing that stuck out for

Jimmy was the moment when Ian Coates had revealed that he wasn't Jimmy's biological father. Jimmy took a deep breath. *It doesn't matter*, he insisted inside his head. *He's nothing to do with me now. Forget his lies.* Jimmy longed to believe the words he was repeating to himself. But underneath it, he could feel a mist of confusion. Britain could never be his home as long as the Neo-democratic Government was in power – his fake father included.

Suddenly, Jimmy felt his muscles tense up. He could hear something. A drone.

"Here it is," announced Froy.

The noise was huge now, and getting louder all the time. The shadow of the plane loomed over them. Then Jimmy saw it – like a sharpened bullet, the EA-22G Growler scythed through the wind. The slim grey fuselage was almost camouflaged against the sky, but the fins were tipped with red and they flashed like flames. Then, with the thunder of the plane touching ground, a glimmer of sunlight caught the emblem on the side of the cockpit – a white star on a navy disc.

Jimmy gasped. For the first time, he was awed by the power of the organisation that was taking care of him now. Colonel Keays hadn't just used his CIA resources – now he'd mobilised the US airforce. Jimmy felt a smile creep over his face, confident that they would be able to escort him anywhere in the world in safety.

But where? Jimmy laughed at his own stupidity. In all the fuss of escaping NJ7 and the trauma of leaving his family behind, he hadn't thought to ask where in the world he was going to be taken.

"Where will it...?" he started, almost overcome by excitement. "I mean, where am I...?"

Froy broke into a huge smile.

"I hope you like Mexican food."

02 *PROTECTED OR HUNTED?*

Felix bent double and pressed his hand into his stomach, trying to ease a stitch.

"Wait," he panted.

"Come on," insisted Georgie, a couple of paces ahead. "We can't stop." She looked around, her face twisted with concern. It was almost fully light now. The shadows no longer offered a place to hide.

"We don't even know where we're running," said Felix, still catching his breath.

"New York's a big place." Georgie replied. "We can disappear. But that safehouse is definitely not safe."

"But where do we sleep? What do we eat? I'm going to need breakfast in a minute and, like, every day for the rest of my life."

"I don't know," said Georgie. She wiped the sweat from her face and Felix noticed her hands were trembling. "We can't let them take us. We can't trust them."

"But we can't just run in no direction at all, can we?" Felix asked. "This is the CIA – if they want us, they'll find us. We've got no chance."

Georgie ignored him. She was searching the street signs.

"We need a hostel or something," she whispered to herself.

"They might even help us," Felix went on. "They helped Jimmy, didn't they?"

"We *think* they've helped Jimmy." Georgie glared at Felix, her eyes full of fear. "But they were meant to be protecting us too. How come NJ7 knew where the safehouse was? If the CIA had been doing their job properly, NJ7 would never have taken your parents."

Felix didn't have an answer for that. It was the last thing he wanted to think about and for Georgie to bring it up was cruel. In his head, Felix could see his mother being forced to the ground by those huge men in black suits. He could picture her face trying to reassure him and at the same time urging him to get away. He thought he could remember his father crying out for him, but he couldn't have actually heard that. By the time Olivia and Neil Muzbeke had been forced into a car, Felix and Georgie had already escaped in the back of a grocery lorry, unseen by the NJ7 agents. Felix's memory was playing tricks.

The wind swept across Manhattan, straight off the sea. Felix shivered.

"I'm sorry," said Georgie, seeing the distress on her friend's face. "I didn't mean to..."

"It's OK. They've been taken before." Felix tried to smile, but his large brown eyes remained full of anxiety. "I think it's their new hobby."

"Wait," said Georgie. "What happened to that map your dad gave you just before... you know..."

Felix's face lit up. He reached into the back pocket of his jeans and pulled out a crumpled leaflet. Their hands scrabbled to open it out. It was a tourist map of Manhattan from the rack in the restaurant beneath the safehouse. It highlighted all of the main attractions and, even better, all the hostels.

"This is perfect," said Georgie. "Let's head there." She stabbed her finger on to the paper, at the north end of Manhattan, in the heart of Harlem.

"That's miles away," said Felix.

"The further from the safehouse the better. Do you have any money on you?"

Felix slapped his pockets, then shook his head.

"Never mind," said Georgie. "We'll think of something."

"Don't worry," Felix reassured her with a cheeky grin. "I always think of something."

They set off at a jog again, weaving through the side streets and back alleys, constantly looking over their shoulders. Manhattan was quiet – it was still too early for anybody to be driving around except a few yellow cabs. But they both knew that within the next hour it would come alive with people and cars. If they were still out on the streets then, they wouldn't be able to spot anybody coming for them until it was too late. They had to get somewhere safe fast.

They rounded another corner, Georgie still running slightly ahead of her friend. With every sound, they imagined the grip of an agent round their necks. In every cab that passed, the driver looked like he was watching them. At the end of their alleyway was a main road. Georgie grabbed the map as they stopped reluctantly. They slipped between a line of dumpsters to be out of sight. The smell was bitter and powerful, but it was the least of their worries.

"Where are we?" she asked, panting hard.

Felix slowly leaned out of the shadows, looking for a street sign.

"Doesn't look like Chinatown any more," he started. "But I'm never—"

Something grabbed him under the arm. He tried to shout, but a hand clamped down over his mouth. Georgie looked up in horror. The breath froze in her throat. Felix had disappeared into the blackness of a doorway opposite. Then a white arm reached out.

Georgie shrank back, but the dumpsters blocked her in. She was trapped. She wanted to scream, but when Georgie opened her mouth, nothing came out. The hand stretched closer, spreading its white fingers into a claw.

Then Georgie realised her breathing had steadied and her heart wasn't pounding. She didn't feel scared any more, but couldn't work out why. Then her brain finally caught up with what her eyes had seen – a wedding ring. It sparkled in the light on the ring finger of the hand in front of her, and it was a ring she recognised.

"Get in here now!" insisted a woman's voice from the doorway opposite.

"Mum!" Georgie whispered, bounding out from between the dumpsters.

"What's going on?" asked Helen Coates, wrapping her arms round her daughter. "Are you OK? And where's Jimmy?"

"He's OK," Felix started, almost breathless with excitement. "He must have planned this whole thing with the CIA without even telling us about it, and then we saw him being shot – but not really shot. And he fell backwards into the river and it really looked like he was dead – but we knew he wasn't, I mean, he isn't, because he left us a message before he did it and we worked it out. It was pretty cool the way he fooled them."

"Wait, slow down," said Helen. "He was *shot*?"

"Yeah," Felix replied. "But it must have been with fake bullets or something."

"So where is he now?"

"If we're right," said Georgie, "then he's with the CIA."

"Of course we're right," Felix insisted.

"So what are you two doing running away from the CIA?"

Georgie and Felix hesitated, and looked at each other. "Have you seen them?" Georgie asked. "Are they really after us?"

Helen wiped her face with her hands. Very slowly, she nodded. "I've been tracking you from the safehouse."

Georgie knew her mother used to be an NJ7 agent herself years and years ago, but she was still impressed.

"You've had two agents on your tail as well," Helen went on. "If they're as good as I think they are, they'll have accessed the satellite surveillance by now. They'll be here any minute."

"So what do we do?" Felix gasped.

"Quick," Georgie whispered. "We should get moving." She was about to dash back out into the alley, but her mother caught her by the arm.

"Wait," said Helen firmly. "Why are you running? What do you know that I don't?"

"The safehouse," Georgie answered straightaway. "These men came and we had to escape. But they got Felix's parents."

"I know," Helen replied. "I saw it all."

"You were there?"

"I couldn't find Chris at the airport, so I was going back to the safehouse. I'd reached the end of the street when I saw the men taking Neil and Olivia. I'm sorry, Felix." She put a hand on his shoulder and crouched down to look in his eyes. "They're going to be OK. We'll find them and sort all of this out. It might take a little time, that's all."

Felix looked away. He didn't like being forced to think about it.

"If the CIA is on our side," he asked, a little break in his voice, "how come NJ7 knew where the safehouse was?"

"I don't know," said Helen. "It could be a million reasons. It might not even have been NJ7."

"What?" Felix gasped.

"I watched those men. Their methods were..." She searched for the right word. "...different. But NJ7 can't have a lot of agents posted in America. Most likely, they had to employ MI6 to do the work. Or..." She paused, as if she didn't want to continue. "Or it could have been the French."

"What?" Georgie exclaimed. "What are the French doing here?"

"Everything they can to stop America helping Britain."

"What have my parents got to do with that?" Felix asked.

"Nothing," Helen sighed. "But the French know about Jimmy. If they can make it look like the CIA failed to protect his friends, they might be hoping Jimmy will turn against America and go back to France."

Felix's face was scrunched up in confusion. "Why can't anything ever be what it looks like?" he whispered.

"You're right," Helen agreed. "Look, what do we know for sure?" She counted off the items on her fingers as she went. "First, the safehouse isn't safe. Second, the area is crawling with agents of all kinds, and third, the CIA is the only organisation likely to protect us."

"OK," Georgie muttered, thinking hard. "I suppose we should go with the CIA. I don't trust them, but at least we'll get more information that way. We can ask them about Jimmy. That's the only way we'll be certain."

"We are certain," Felix insisted. "There's no way Jimmy would let himself be shot like that unless it was on purpose."

"OK, Felix," Helen reassured him. "I'm sure you're right. But in any case, the best way to find out whether we can trust Colonel Keays and his agents is to keep them close. If we run, we'll never know if they want to protect us or kill us."

Georgie drew in a deep breath and took a long look at Felix.

"I suppose they were going to catch us soon anyway," she said. "There's no way two kids can hide from the CIA."

"I disagree." A man's voice with a New York accent interrupted them. Georgie and Felix spun round to see a thin, chiselled man leaning casually on the dumpster opposite. He was wearing a plain black suit. "I thought you were doing a pretty good job."

Then he put his mouth to his lapel and whispered into a small microphone, "We got 'em."

03 NEPTUNE'S SHADOW

At 800 kilometres an hour it can be hard to make out
what somebody's saying to you. Jimmy shifted the
earpiece in his helmet. It obviously wasn't designed to
fit the head of an eleven-year-old. The wind and the
plane's engine combined to create a powerful roar.
Jimmy wanted to concentrate on looking for a break in
the clouds beneath them. Every now and again they
offered a glimpse of an incredible sight: America's
east coast from 13,000 metres up. But the Growler
wasn't designed for passengers to enjoy the view.
With all the dials and switches packed around him,
Jimmy found it hard to see anything outside the plane
except miles and miles of bright, empty sky.

The plane had only four seats, set out two by two.
Jimmy was strapped in tight directly behind Froy. Next
to Froy was the pilot, another CIA agent whose name
Jimmy didn't know. He couldn't even see the man's

face from where he was sitting, just some wild strands of black curly hair creeping out from under his helmet. The seat next to Jimmy was empty.

In the three hours since the pilot had picked up his new passengers, he and Froy had done nothing but argue.

"I told you," Agent Froy shouted into his headset, "there weren't any other planes available."

"So because the hangars were empty you decided to pluck a ride out of the sky?" The pilot's voice was gruff and Jimmy placed his accent from one of the Southern states. "This isn't American Airlines. I'm not here to take you and some kid on vacation."

Jimmy gritted his teeth. He didn't want to get involved – he was just pleased that at last they were getting well away from New York. But Froy was steaming.

"You want me to tell Colonel Keays you're giving us grief?" he yelled.

"Don't you get it?" came the other agent's retort. "This plane is still on an operation! I haven't delivered my package!"

"Give me a break, Bligh," Froy sighed. "You're on your way home, you needed to refuel anyway and you were up in the air again in under a minute. What's your problem?"

"My problem? First of all, I'm not on my way 'home'. I'm on my way to the data analysis centre in Miami. To drop you over sunny *Me-hi-co* is a 2500-mile round trip out of our way."

"Excuse me," Jimmy asked meekly, "Did you say drop us *over*, or drop us *off*?"

"I said drop over and I meant drop over, kid. That's a parachute strapped to your back."

Jimmy felt the square pack pressing into his shoulder blades and felt like an idiot for asking.

"And that's another thing." Bligh took a deep breath then blew straight on. "This is a *spy* plane. I'm meant to stay above observable altitude. That's above radar, above the clouds, above everything. I was meant to refuel in-flight and I'll have to drop again so you can make the jump to the ground. But coming down sucks! The minute I dip low enough you can forget about the enemy needing radar. My grandmother could have seen us back there – and she's blind!"

The more Jimmy heard, the more surprised he was at how disorganised the arrangements were.

"OK, OK," said Froy with a sigh. "Stop busting my—"

BANG!

The plane gave a massive jolt. Jimmy was hurled to the left and his helmet slammed against the side of the cockpit. He heard both agents yelling through his headset, but he couldn't make out what they were saying. The whole plane was violently shaking. Jimmy's stomach rolled around. Then he heard the first clear words through his earpiece.

"It's there!" Bligh shouted. His reedy voice came as

a shock. Jimmy strained against his strap to see what the man was talking about.

"On your DS!" said Froy urgently. "Your display station!"

Jimmy looked down at the screen in front of him. It was about thirty centimetres square and in full colour. There was a green outline of jagged straight lines surrounded by blue. Jimmy assumed that represented the coastline beneath them. The whole screen was criss-crossed by thin blue and red lines, but it was hard to make anything out because of the furious vibrations of the plane.

"It sprung out of nowhere!" Bligh cried. "They won't miss next time." Then Jimmy saw it – first the black aeroplane icon that represented the plane he was sitting in. Then, barely two centimetres away on the screen, the flashing red dot that could only mean trouble.

"They've found me!" Jimmy gasped, barely able to get the words out of his throat. "How did they find me?"

"Hold on tight!" Bligh screamed.

For a second Jimmy felt like the plane had disappeared from under him. Every organ inside him was thrown into his throat. Bligh had sent them into a rapid dive.

"You?" said the man suddenly. "Why do you think they're after you?"

The plane pulled out of the dive with a sudden

swoop. The massive reversal of the G-force thrust Jimmy deep into his seat. Blood rushed to his head and it felt like his brain was about to burst.

"I don't know how they found us," Froy shouted, peering behind him through the glass. "I'm sorry, Jimmy." Jimmy looked over as well. With the intense shaking and the limited view, he only caught sight of it for a split-second, but it was enough – the wing tip of another plane. It was behind them, it was fast and it could only be NJ7.

"This is nothing to do with you!" yelled Bligh, still grappling with the controls of the plane.

"It's NJ7," Froy replied. "They're after Jimmy. Look, their plane has a green stripe on the side. That's their emblem. You Brits are too damn arrogant to do anything in secret, aren't you, Jimmy?"

Jimmy blanked out the voices. He needed his body to respond to the danger. He closed his eyes, searching for that power inside him. He had to forget that he was terrified – that was only the human part of him, the 38 per cent that was a normal, frightened boy.

"No," Bligh announced suddenly. "It's not possible. There's no way they could know you were on this plane and co-ordinate an attack so quickly. We're only a few miles outside American airspace. They must have been tracking this plane. They're not here for you,

Jimmy. They're after me. As soon as we dipped below safe altitude to pick you up, they spotted us easily."

At last, Jimmy felt a rush up the side of his neck – like a rising flood taking over his brain and energising every muscle. His breathing slowed. The panic in his chest crumpled into a harmless ball. With that, he suddenly had the confidence to take in what Bligh was saying.

"What do you mean?" he yelled, his voice now infused with authority. "Why are they after you? You mentioned your 'package' before – what did you mean? What's your mission?"

There was no response, though Jimmy knew Bligh had heard him. He could see the man's shoulders tighten.

They surged onwards, back up above the clouds. The vibrations calmed a little and Bligh kept deploying what countermeasures he could. Without even thinking about it, Jimmy knew that first he would send out a hot flare to divert heat-seeking missiles, then chaff – debris that would disrupt any missile that automatically sought the nearest solid objects.

"Can't we fire back?" Froy shouted.

Jimmy didn't wait for the pilot to answer. His voice came out low and calm. Inside, he was thrilled at his own conviction.

"This is an Electronic Countermeasures plane, not an attack plane. Our missiles can take out anti-radar artillery systems and surface-to-air missiles on land or on ships over a hundred kilometres away. But we've got no way of attacking another plane."

Now Jimmy turned back to Bligh. His eyes seared into the back of the man's helmet. "If you want to survive, I need all the information," he demanded. "You said they must have tracked you. Where from? What were you doing? What was your mission? Tell me NOW!"

The plane rocked again.

"We're losing control!" Froy screamed, above the rattle of the metal struts. They were barely holding the cabin together.

"OK," Bligh yelled at last. "You're right – I need to tell you. But not to survive – to complete the mission." He frantically punched some keys on his display station. "God, I hope this CPU is still working. Can you see that?"

Jimmy looked at his own screen. Aerial photographs flashed up in front of him, one after the other. Jimmy was amazed at their detail – he knew they must have been taken from thousands of metres up and with the plane travelling at speed.

"This is Neptune's Shadow," Bligh announced, rushing to get the words out, "the second-largest oil rig in the world." His voice shook with the vibrations of the plane, but Jimmy wondered whether it was fear as well. "It's 250 kilometres off the east coast of England, in the North Sea."

Jimmy watched the images flash up, faster and faster, desperately trying to hold on to any of them in his head. Still the plane shook and rattled. Jimmy could barely hear what Bligh was saying.

"This is your precious package?" Froy bellowed. He was furious. "This is what was so important you couldn't divert to pick us up? A damn oil rig?"

"It's not an oil rig," Bligh snapped back. "That's what I found out. And NJ7 will do anything to stop me getting back with this intelligence. Neptune's Shadow is a secret missile base disguised as a massive oil rig. And these pictures show that its rockets are trained on France. The Brits are preparing a strike on Paris."

Jimmy felt his gut twisting into a rope.

"Does anybody know about this?" he gasped.

"Just us three and the Government of Great Britain," replied Bligh. "We're too far out of range for me to radio it. The only place this information is stored is on the CPU of this aeroplane and inside our heads. And to be honest, it doesn't look like this plane is going to be around much longer. If something happens..." he paused and cleared his throat. "If we go down... Whoever survives... you have to take this information back to Colonel Keays. He has to know. He has to stop them."

CRASH!

Suddenly, it felt like being in a toy plane whacked by

a sledgehammer. A direct hit. Jimmy was thrown to the side, slamming his head against the wall of the cockpit again. If it hadn't been for the helmet, his skull would have been crushed.

Then the plane went into tailspin.

04 DEATH SPIRAL

Jimmy saw every colour blend into every other. The universe whirled around him, like he was trapped in a tumble dryer – one that was falling to earth at over a hundred metres a second.

Only one thing went through his mind – *Bligh has lost control*. The man was shaking the flight stick frantically and clawing at the switches on the flight panel.

Jimmy looked up, straight ahead out of the cockpit. What he saw numbed the feeling in his entire body. The sea was rushing towards them. Even in the split-second that he stared, the froth on the surface became clearer. He was close enough to see the debris that bobbed on the waves.

Then he looked to the control panel. It was like the most complicated games console in the world. Suddenly, it was as if Jimmy could see through the metal, into the workings of the plane. In a single flash of thought, he could trace the wires behind every button and switch – thousands of them all at once.

"Do exactly what I say!" Jimmy yelled, fighting hard to stop himself blacking out.

"What?" Bligh shouted back in disbelief.

"Kill the engines!" Jimmy ordered. There was such authority in his voice that Bligh did as he was told. The two Pratt and Whitney P450 turbojets fell silent, leaving only the intense scream of the air rushing past the cockpit.

Jimmy's hands tore at his strap. He unclipped his parachute, heaved it off his back and strapped it round the display station of the empty seat next to him. Then he engaged the seat's ejector mechanism. Almost instantly, a section of the cockpit screen popped open and the seat was hurled from the plane. Jimmy saw it slam into the wing as it rotated around them. He was relieved that neither Bligh nor Froy had panicked and tried to eject themselves.

"What are you doing?" screamed Bligh.

Jimmy didn't respond. Instead, he pulled the ripcord on his parachute. The black satin canopy billowed into the sky behind them. The resistance would only slow their fall by a fraction – the 'chute was designed to carry a single human, not a fighter jet. But it would grant them an extra split-second, which could be enough. The canopy behind them would also serve a second purpose.

"Release the internal fuel supply!" Jimmy commanded. Bligh didn't hesitate. A trail of black liquid streamed behind them, making the plane lighter by the second, and filling the parachute canopy with petroleum fumes.

There was no time to issue another order. Jimmy reached over to the controls himself, flicked the safety cover from the missile switch and jammed his thumb on the orange button.

He didn't need to take aim. He knew that without a specifically programmed target, the AGM-99 would automatically seek out the largest solid object within its scope. He just hoped that one of the logs in the water would be big enough to register.

A single missile flamed through the sky ahead of them, twisting in the direction of its target. Ten centimetres either side and the missile would have plunged hundreds of metres beneath the waves before exploding. But it hit the log right in the centre. Up came a blast of red and black flame, heating the air immediately around it by hundreds of degrees and igniting the fumes caught in the parachute.

The updraft was enough to push the Growler out of its spiral.

"Now!" Jimmy yelled. Bligh knew exactly what Jimmy meant. That moment he re-ignited the engines. The roar returned. The silk canopy behind them was incinerated instantly and they swooped along the surface of the water.

Jimmy couldn't help smiling.

"Good flying, kid," Bligh gasped, lifting them back into the clouds at hundreds of kilometres an hour. "But it's not over." He tapped his display unit. The red flashing dot was still on the screen and it was closing in. Jimmy was amazed that the man still sounded so calm.

"We'd better eject," said Jimmy, constantly manoeuvring the plane so they couldn't be shot at. "The plane's damaged and we're out of fuel. If we're not hit first, we'll crash anyway."

But then Bligh looked across at Froy.

"Froy!" he cried, shaking his CIA colleague by the arm. "He's unconscious, Jimmy! I'm not ejecting without him." Bligh reached across to check the other CIA man's pulse. "Here, you take this." He unclipped his parachute and passed it back to Jimmy.

Jimmy pulled the straps of the parachute pack over his arms.

"I'll fasten myself to Froy," Bligh went on, feeling for one of the hooks on his belt. "I'll get us both out and I'll pull the cord on his 'chute."

Jimmy was about to follow the agent's instructions, but his hand hesitated over the eject mechanism. He glanced again at the red dot on his screen. *Come on*, he told himself. *Get out of here.* But there was a dark force inside him, stopping his muscles going through with action.

"They'll see me," Jimmy gasped suddenly. "I can't jump out. If an NJ7 pilot sees a boy coming out of this plane, the information will get back to Miss Bennett. She'll know it's me. The whole operation will be for nothing."

"Who's Miss Bennett?"

"She's the head of NJ7. I can't let her know I'm still alive."

"It's too late for that!" Bligh yelled. "We've got to go. I can't eject until you've gone – I'm flying this thing!"

But still Jimmy held back. In his head was a human cry, willing him to eject from the plane. His programming swamped it.

"No," he announced. "We can get rid of them."

Determination tensed his face.

"We can't!" Bligh screamed. "They've…"

His voice faded. Jimmy looked up. Through the black grime on the glass, he saw a missile burning towards them. All his muscles seemed to melt in fear.

"Hold Froy!" he screamed.

But Bligh wasn't moving. The high-pitched whine of the missile grew louder. Jimmy stared at its black point, bearing down on them.

"Come on! I'm wearing your parachute!"

"It's up to you, Jimmy," said Bligh quietly. Jimmy could barely hear his voice. "There's nobody else." The man turned round and Jimmy saw his face for the first time. His skin was dark and his eyes were commanding. "Get back to Colonel Keays. Tell him about the missile base, Jimmy. Someone has to stop Neptune's Shadow."

SMACK!

The missile hit the nose of the Growler. Jimmy felt himself thrust forwards, as if they'd flown into a brick wall. His hands jumped to his face and he squeezed his eyes shut. His helmet smashed the back of Froy's seat. When he opened his eyes, for a split-second he caught sight of Bligh's face again. A large shard of glass was sticking out of the agent's cheek, just below his eye.

"Neptune's Shadow!" the man bellowed. Jimmy reached out to catch him, but too late.

BOOM!

The plane disintegrated in a massive explosion. Jimmy was thrown into the air. He felt the cold wind and the burning metal blasting into him at the same time. He desperately tried to keep his eyes open, searching for Bligh and Froy. *They're going to die*, he told himself. In his panic, he thought he saw them falling through the debris, one with a parachute on his back but unconscious, the other completely helpless.

Neptune's Shadow! Jimmy heard Bligh's last words in his ears over and over again, above the din of the air rushing past him as he hurtled down through the atmosphere.

The noise was matched by the turmoil in Jimmy's head. *I could have saved them*, he thought. *Why did I hesitate? Why did I take his parachute?*

Parachute... The word seemed to reawaken Jimmy's programming. It would never forgot its first priority – to stay alive. While his mind was in chaos, his hands moved calmly and expertly to the ripcord. Even while he wanted to scream, free-falling through the carnage, he could hear a quiet voice in his head counting to ten. Then he felt his arm go tense and suddenly everything changed.

It felt as if his whole body was jerked upwards. The parachute burst open above him. The roar of the wind in his ears changed to the sound of a breeze. Bits of the plane still dropped around him, but soon he was far above them, floating down towards the sea.

05 TERMINAL INTENTION

Mitchell Glenthorne stalked through Terminal One of New York's JFK airport, limping slightly. His shoulders were broad for a thirteen-year-old, but they were hunched over, masking the size and strength in his chest. His face was fixed in a scowl. The inside of his head was nothing but a jumble of silent curses. He was passing the time by running through a list of all the people he wished he could have it out with. It took in most of the people he had ever met, starting with his brother Lenny and his parents.

He thought of Lenny, lying on a slab somewhere in London, being kept alive by NJ7 for experimental purposes. *Serves him right*, he thought. Mitchell's parents' only fault had been to die in a car crash when he was a baby, but now he had reason to doubt these family relationships.

Jimmy Coates, the renegade assassin – the *dead*

renegade assassin, Mitchell corrected in his head – had claimed before he was shot that Mitchell and Jimmy were half-brothers. If that were true, where did that leave Mitchell's parents and Lenny?

Now wasn't the time to work it out, so instead he snorted at how ridiculous the idea was. He blocked out the thought that his whole existence was ridiculous. From his appearance, no one would have believed that he was the first 38 per cent human, organic assassin. Or that he'd been called on to enter active service five years before he was due to be fully operational.

He held the image of Jimmy's face in his imagination a second longer, as if out of some kind of respect for the dead. Actually, it was to give Jimmy a double dose of cursing. Jimmy was the one who had given Mitchell this limp. He'd be walking normally again in no time, but still, every faltering stride gave him another reason to sneer at the memory of Jimmy Coates.

The airport terminal was busy as usual and, as usual, it was saturated with security personnel. Hardly even thinking about it, Mitchell noted their positions and sightlines as he passed each one. After he had made his move, he would have to escape the building. These armed men and women would be in his way.

Next on the list of people he was fed up with was Miss Bennett. She was technically his boss, but always seemed to act like a sarcastic schoolteacher towards him. Instead of praising him for his part in the termination of Jimmy Coates, she had immediately dispatched him to continue his ongoing mission to find and kill Zafi. She hadn't even given him time for his knee to heal.

And that brought him to Zafi. Mitchell took up a position overlooking the Air France check-in desks, lying in wait for his target. Zafi was the organic assassin designed and built by the French Secret Service twelve years before. That made her almost two years younger than Mitchell, but so far Mitchell had to admit that her speed and ingenuity had got the better of him. But that wasn't even what he minded the most about her. He could have respected Zafi if she'd acted with the discipline and seriousness that Mitchell always tried to bring to his job. But she never did.

Agency computers had flagged up a last-minute reservation on a transatlantic flight, under the name 'Michelle Glenthorne'. Mitchell knew that Zafi was taunting him by booking herself a flight in that name. He clenched his fists. As soon as Zafi dared to turn up, no matter what disguise she tried, Mitchell was ready to rip her head off. That's how annoyed he felt.

Zafi peeked through the curtain of the fitting room of the Ferragamo outlet. The clothes were too fancy for her tastes and they didn't make anything in her size, but that wasn't why she was here. As soon as she saw Mitchell she gave a light giggle. She laughed again when she noticed how annoyed he looked, and how hard he was studying the faces of everybody who went anywhere near the Air France check-in desks.

She slipped out of the fitting room and took a pink pashmina scarf to the till. Without looking up, the middle-aged woman behind the desk asked, "How will you pay?"

"Charge it to the Stovorsky account," Zafi instructed confidently.

The woman shuddered slightly and her eyes jumped to her customer's face. Zafi pouted. "Of course," said the woman, nervously fingering the gold chains round her neck. She lifted the coin tray in the till and pulled out a selection of half a dozen airline tickets. Her hands were trembling as she fanned them on the desk.

"Get them out of sight," Zafi snapped.

The woman gasped and shoved her hands back in the till.

"Is this Icelandic wool?" Zafi asked loudly, feeling the pashmina between her thumb and fingers. The woman took another corner of the scarf and felt it the same way.

"It's the finest quality," she announced.

"But too expensive for me," Zafi replied and swept out of the shop. In her hand was the ticket that the woman had passed her under the scarf. It was a small charter flight, destination: Reykjavik, Iceland. The passenger name was 'Glenthornia Mitchell'.

06 SUSPICION

Colonel Keays was shaped like a box and his chest was a tapestry of medals, with ribbons in every different colour against the dark blue material of his uniform. He stood tall and proud, with his chin slightly raised and his cap under his arm. The stark light of the room reflected off the parts of his head where the hair was at its thinnest.

He looked over the three people standing in front of him and for a long time there was silence. Georgie and Felix stood on either side of Georgie's mum, shifting from foot to foot. Helen Coates herself seemed completely relaxed, staring straight back at Keays.

A small team of CIA agents had brought them deep into the basement of Sak's Fifth Avenue Department Store. But the ornate interior of the shop floor was a world away. They had found themselves surrounded by the stormy grey of completely bare concrete walls, facing the US Director of Intelligence, while three other agents waited outside.

For no apparent reason, Keays snorted a short

laugh, though he wasn't smiling. "I'm glad we found you first," he announced. "The streets were still crawling with NJ7 agents when my men picked you up. But don't worry; this is America. Miss Bennett knows she can't do anything here unless I give her the OK."

"You know Miss Bennett?" Felix blurted.

"Of course. Intelligence agencies all over the world have to talk to each other, don't we? Especially countries like Britain and America. Countries that used to be close." He paused and looked at them hard. "It's a shame we're not so close any more."

"A shame for who?" Helen muttered.

"Ha!" Keays laughed properly this time. "You tell me – do British people like not being allowed to buy American products?"

"Do American companies like not being allowed to sell them?" Helen's voice was soft yet full of confidence.

"We used to protect you," Keays insisted.

"We used to fight your wars," said Helen. "Times change."

"And so do people," Keays replied quickly. "I understand you used to work for NJ7 yourself, Mrs Coates?"

Helen nodded slowly. "I... retired."

"And yet your husband appears to have been promoted."

Helen dropped her chin to her chest and Felix noticed her fingers automatically twisting her wedding ring. "Please," she began, her voice cracking slightly for the first time, "just tell me what happened to Jimmy."

"You should be very proud, Mrs Coates." Keays spoke quietly and quickly. "Your son is a remarkably intelligent young man, quite apart from his unique skills. Yes, he's alive. He wanted me to make sure you knew that, even though it could jeopardise the safety of all of you. As long as Miss Bennett is sure that Jimmy is dead, you'll be safe."

Huge smiles burst out on the faces of his visitors. Helen breathed a massive sigh of relief and gripped Georgie's hand.

"Not so tight," Georgie whispered, but she didn't really mind. She looked across and beamed at Felix, who was almost bouncing on the spot with delight.

"Thank you, Colonel," said Helen.

Suddenly, Felix's mood changed. "What about the safehouse?" he asked. "Not very safe, was it? It was rubbish." He narrowed his eyes and folded his arms. "You don't even care, do you? They took my..." He didn't finish his sentence. "You were meant to be protecting us."

"He's right," Helen jumped in. "Felix could have expressed it a little more politely," she gave him a quick glare, "but we do have to know what's going on. If the CIA spends so much time talking to NJ7, is it possible one of your agents was talking about something they shouldn't have been?"

Keays exploded with another short, sharp laugh. It echoed round the room. "Ha! A leak!" He shook his head quickly. "Impossible. I've got to tell you, Felix," he stared into the boy's eyes, "I don't blame you for being mad. It makes me mad too, and I'm not the one whose parents are being held by NJ7 right now. To be honest, I don't even know what they plan to do with them. They can't use them against Jimmy, because as far as they know Jimmy is dead. Maybe it's a kind of insurance. I don't know. But it's something I'd like to find out."

Felix was about to jump in with another question, but Keays cut him off. "And no, I have no idea how the security of the safehouse was breached. I have people looking into it right now. But one thing is for sure – double agents don't exist any more. There is nobody in the CIA leaking classified information to NJ7. It's a tactic that's just too messy. The Russians demonstrated that for everybody back in the Cold War. It's more likely to be from electronic espionage, or from one of their operatives working on American soil. We'll have to tighten up our systems, that's all."

The colonel winked and it sent a shudder down Felix's spine. He had the urge to spit, but managed to stop himself. Instead, he gave a deliberately over-the-top smile and a huge wink of his own.

"There's good news as well, though," Keays went on.

"Are you sending us back to the UK?" Helen asked, her voice sombre.

Keays nodded.

"What?" said Georgie and Felix together.

"I thought you would," said Helen. "It's for the best. We can look for Felix's parents." She ruffled his hair into an even more chaotic state than it was normally. "And find Chris too." Her smile dissolved.

"Jimmy did what he did so that the rest of you wouldn't have to be on the run for the rest of your lives," Keays explained. "Realistically, we'd never be able to hide you as a family. It's much harder than hiding just one person and NJ7 have the best resources in the world. They'd find you."

"But now they think Jimmy's dead," said Georgie, "we have to go back to Britain?"

"Right." Keays clapped his hands together. He sounded far too cheerful. "It's time to go home!"

"Won't Miss Bennett try to kill us again?"

"Ha! Don't worry. She's got no reason to hurt you now. And anyway, I can talk to her. I'll sort everything out and you can be on a plane home by this afternoon."

"What will you tell her?" Georgie asked.

"Don't worry about it. You guys will be fully briefed and have a complete cover story. It'll probably be something like this: you were all arrested for being in the US illegally. The authorities here obviously want to send you back to Britain, but I have to check with Miss Bennett whether you're going to be in danger if that goes ahead. We're not allowed to send people back home to be killed. If I know Miss Bennett at all, she'll jump at this. She'd much rather have you under her nose where she can watch you, than see you thrown in prison over here."

"Thrown in prison?" Georgie gasped.

"You wouldn't really be, understand," Keays quickly reassured her. "That's just what Miss Bennett will think."

Georgie nodded slowly. She was still far from certain that she should trust this man and she hated that he was so light-hearted. "Mum," she said, trying to hold back tears.

"What's the matter?" asked Helen, crouching down to take her daughter's face in her hands. Georgie shivered at her touch.

"Don't you know?" Georgie's voice was unsteady and full of anger. Her mother just looked at her in astonishment, eyes wide. "How can you go ahead with this as if everything's great? It's never going to go back to normal, is it?"

"It won't be normal exactly," Helen said softly, "but we'll get by. This is the only way. We'll be able to have a life again."

"Yeah," scoffed Georgie. "Some life – with Dad running the country now as some kind of dictator. I suppose that's OK, isn't it?" Her voice was growing more and more sarcastic, and tears brimmed in her eyes. "And how can you act like it's OK that we're never going to see Jimmy again?"

Helen pulled her daughter towards her, but Georgie held back.

"We will see him again," Helen insisted. "It might not be for a long time, but we will see him. One day we'll all be back together. For the time being, isn't it better that we're alive and safe? Isn't that better than running across the world with NJ7 trying to kill us every second of the day? That's why Jimmy did this. He did it so we could stop running. You need to be back at school, getting on with your life, spending time with your friends... We need to go home."

Georgie wiped her eyes. "How will it be home without Jimmy? And without Dad?"

"We have to try."

"You don't even remember," Georgie mumbled.

"Remember what?"

Georgie stared at her mother for a long time, her face full of bitterness. Then she looked past her, to Felix.

After a long pause, Felix's face lit up. "Oh my God!" he gasped. "You mean his birthday, right?"

Georgie nodded. "It's next week."

Helen stood up and ran her hands through her hair. "Is it nearly April already?" she whispered. "I guess with everything else I didn't notice the date."

"I haven't got him a present," Felix blurted out.

"Of course you haven't," said Georgie. "When have we had time for shopping?"

"Yeah, but, you know, a birthday's a birthday, even if you are on the run from the Secret Service. You know what? I think they should have some kind of rule that nobody is allowed to try to kill you on your birthday." Georgie rolled her eyes. Once Felix got started, there was no point trying to stop him. "And if you do try to kill someone on their birthday, they should be allowed to keep all your presents when it's your birthday. And your cards. No wait, you can keep your cards. Nobody wants cards anyway. So just the presents."

"You're a nutcase," Georgie mumbled – but a smile had crept on to her face. Felix was bursting with energy again and bouncing on the spot.

He turned to Colonel Keays. "Can we send Jimmy a card?" he asked suddenly. "It can be secret. Nobody has to know about it but us. And Jimmy, obviously. And you can give it to him. You can, can't you?"

Colonel Keays was taken aback. "Jimmy's deep in hiding," he mumbled. "A team of agents is making sure nobody knows who he is. He's officially dead."

"But he can still have a birthday, can't he?"

Keays shook his head in wonder and let out a deep chuckle. "Jimmy's lucky to have a friend like you," he announced, "and a sister who loves him as much as you do, Georgie." He paused to think for a second, then went on, "I don't think we should start sending cards to people who are meant to be dead. It's not good to have anything identifiable lying around that might give the game away to NJ7. But how about you write Jimmy a message? Don't sign though. Don't even write his name on it. I'll make sure Jimmy gets it."

He pulled out a notepad and a pencil from his inside pocket.

"Wicked," Felix beamed. "I'm going to write him the funniest birthday message ever."

"Wait," said Georgie, "I'll give you a hand." She moved towards Felix, but her eyes were studying Colonel Keays. "Let's write it together." She took the pencil and a sheet of paper from Keays. "Colonel Keays," she said quietly. "Can I ask you something?"

"Of course."

"Why did you help us escape from Britain in the first place, if you were just going to send us back?"

"I'm sending you back now that it's safe," Keays explained, his expression completely blank.

"You mean, now that we don't have Jimmy – and you do?"

Keays didn't move. His eyes locked on to Georgie's. "Write your message," he said, pushing the paper into Georgie's hand. "And have a good flight home."

Georgie and Felix huddled over the sheet of paper in a corner of the room.

"Thank you, Colonel," said Helen. "I know they seem... ungrateful, but your help means a lot to us."

Keays nodded silently. Then Georgie spun round, waving the paper above her head.

"OK, we're done. Do you want to add something, Mum?" She thrust the paper into her mother's hand. Helen examined it as if she'd never seen a page of writing before. Her whole body seemed to freeze. Georgie held out the pencil, but noticed that her mum's lips were trembling.

"It's OK," said Georgie, "I'll put 'love from Mum' or something at the bottom." She pulled the pencil back towards her. Helen Coates turned away, wiping her eyes.

"Don't worry," said Keays. "Your son did the right thing. It's better this way. For everyone. Jimmy is going to be fine. You have my promise."

"Where is he now?" Helen whispered.

"I can't tell you."

"Where is he?" Helen insisted. "I need to know where my son is."

"At this moment, Jimmy is absolutely fine." Keays took the note from Georgie, folded it carefully and slipped it into his pocket. "I absolutely guarantee it. Jimmy is happy and Jimmy is safe."

07 SUSHI FOR ONE

Jimmy's legs hit the water and his whole body pitched forwards. Huge waves lifted him up, then sucked him down again. With incredible force he was pulled under the surface. His breathing was so fast he was afraid his heart might stop. But he wasn't panicking. He unclipped his parachute and kicked out with his legs, desperately trying to stop his whole body going numb. He could feel the cold scratching at his bones.

His programming surged through him, controlling his muscles. It would never let him give in to the cold or the water. He was at least two metres under the surface now. Salt water stung his eyes, but Jimmy kept them open. At last another of his amazing capabilities was kicking in: his in-built night-vision enhanced the light. The underwater world took on a rich, blue haze. Jimmy would have been lost without it. Now he was able to fight towards the surface.

The ocean churned with such force that Jimmy felt like he was a sock in a washing machine. He wanted to thrash his limbs. He wanted to panic, but his body wouldn't let him. Instead, his arms and legs moved calmly, with a maximum of precision and efficiency. His assassin's programming guided him back to the surface within thirty seconds.

His arms wrapped themselves over one of the largest fragments of the plane's fuselage. The air trapped underneath it supported Jimmy's weight. He flopped his chest on to it, clutching it as the waves threw him around like a shuttlecock.

Jimmy's lower half still dangled in the water and he kept his legs moving in a vain fight against the cold. Every few seconds he wiped his eyes. Through the spray, he could see the carpet of flaming debris spread out across the water. Beyond that was a vast empty space, stretching out between him and the horizon. It was overwhelming. But only for a second – then a wave as strong as a wall jumped up to block his view.

There were thoughts racing through his head that sounded like an overheard conversation at the end of a crackling phone line. Hardly understanding it, he was reading the current. He hauled himself completely on to the makeshift raft, steadying himself on his hands and knees.

Gradually, he reached for more fragments of debris, building up a little shelter around him. Then he heaved on the parachute that was swelling in the waves. It took all his strength to gather it in, but eventually he dumped an armful of soaking black silk on to the metal in front of him. Still the wind and the waves buffeted Jimmy around. He had to grip the piece of the plane's fuselage with his knees, while he went about ripping up the parachute.

Every few seconds, a part of him wanted to give up. His limbs were straining just to keep him from falling off his raft back into the water. But something inside him kept him going. Maybe it was programming or maybe it was his human hunger to stay alive. Eventually, he managed to tie half of his parachute across his raft, fastened on each side to a fragment of the aeroplane. He had a sail.

In a few minutes, the sea would consume almost every scrap of what remained of the plane. There'd be hardly any evidence that they'd ever gone down there. But what about the people on board? Was Jimmy the only survivor?

"Hello!?" he shouted. His voice was lost against the crash of the waves and the wind. "Anyone there!?" he screamed, pouring out every last crumb of energy. Tears mixed with the spray of the ocean. He clenched his fists and pounded his metal raft, cursing the forces inside him.

Maybe if his genetics hadn't taken over from his

common sense, the agents would have had a chance. But the assassin in Jimmy hadn't wanted to be seen by NJ7. Jimmy's programming had overcome his human protests. It had saved him, but at the others' expense. It was driven by the most selfish instinct of an assassin: self-protection at all costs.

He could feel it inside him now. It purred while his human self longed to scream at the wind. *I killed them*, he thought. How could they possibly have survived the fall from a plane without an open parachute? *They were trying to save me and I killed them.* How could he have let his programming do it? The second his human instinct had given in, he had condemned two agents.

I won't give in again, Jimmy told himself. *You won't control me.* From now on, he insisted, he would do everything he could to make his programming serve his human intuition. *I control me.*

He curled up, used some of the parachute to tie himself down and pulled the rest completely over him. It would give him a vital extra layer of protection against the sun and the wind. All he could do now was preserve his energy. He knew that the plane had been flying over the coastline. Had they crashed close enough to land to be washed ashore? If not, without food and water, Jimmy knew he would die.

With the black silk covering his face, his world was

completely dark. He closed his eyes and felt the waves surging beneath him.

Jimmy was suddenly aware of a burning sensation on his face. He opened his eyes, then immediately shut them again. The sun was too bright and the parachute must have slipped off his face. How long had he been asleep? His mouth was so dry he thought his tongue might stick to the back of his teeth. *Am I dead?* he thought. *No – too much pain.* Every muscle ached, especially his belly, and when he squinted, the skin around his eyes stung.

It was only now that he realised why he had woken up – the roll of the sea had stopped. He had reached land. He didn't dare move. Where was he? Faint noises invaded his thoughts. Then they grew louder. Slowly, his brain was coming back to consciousness. There were seagulls above him. Their squawks were like sirens telling him to move. He was too exposed. He could be anywhere in the world and anybody could be watching him.

A huge pelican flapped down and perched next to Jimmy's left ear. Still Jimmy couldn't gather the energy to move. *Water* – that was his next thought. *Water or I'll die.* The pelican stabbed its beak into Jimmy's hair. Suddenly, energy seemed to explode into Jimmy's muscles. His arm thrust out so quickly the pelican never saw it coming. Jimmy stabbed his finger and thumb into the base of the bird's neck, pinching its gullet.

In a flurry of feathers and panicked squawks, the pelican choked up one of the fish stored in its massive beak, then flapped away in a hurry.

"Sorry, mate," Jimmy muttered. His voice was so hoarse he hardly recognised it and his throat burned. Gingerly, Jimmy rolled off his raft. His back screamed in pain when he moved, but he had no choice. The helmet weighed his head down, so he pulled it off.

He landed on wet sand and looked up for the first time. He was on a deserted beach. There were no buildings, just large dunes with long tufts of grass. A few hundred metres up the shoreline he could see some fishing boats tied to a small jetty, but they were too far away to make out the language of any writing on them. He still didn't know what country he was in.

When he tried to get to his feet his vision blurred and his head started pounding. But he refused to black out. He could feel his programming rumbling inside him, wrapped around every nerve ending. He knew what it was urging him to do.

He slumped back to his knees and scooped the fish off the sand in front of him, picking up a shell at the same time. In swift, confident movements, his hands went about the painstaking process of scraping the scales off the fish. It took less than a minute.

Then he dug the corner of the shell under the fish's neck and forced a slit down its entire belly. With his fingers, he carefully scooped out the guts. Blood and entrails slopped all over his hand, still warm. The smell was putrid, but Jimmy didn't care. It was vital sustenance. He closed his eyes and started sucking the flesh off the fish's bones. In normal life he was sure it would have tasted gross, but right now his taste buds were almost dead. There was enough fish meat here, and enough precious juice, to keep him alive for the moment.

When he had swallowed all his stomach could take, which wasn't a lot, he turned back to his raft. He ripped down the sail. Then he used every trace of strength to scratch at the markings on the metal. If he left a piece of the US airforce on a public beach, there would be questions asked. Fortunately, there wasn't a lot of work to do – just a serial number that Jimmy quickly bashed out of shape, using a large stone as a mallet. He buried his helmet in the sand, once he'd scratched off the airforce emblem.

The wind whipped off the ocean, blustering his hair around his ears. The tide formed puddles around his knees, but at least the air was warm and the sun had already started drying his skin.

When he'd finished, Jimmy knew he had to move. He was too exposed here. He longed to run, but his body forced him to walk. It took huge effort to move his limbs and even more effort to make it look like he was strolling casually. Running, limping or anything else would have looked conspicuous.

At last he reached the other side of the dunes and found himself on a quiet street with no cars. Across the road was a line of large houses, each one with fancy decking that looked out across the beach. Jimmy felt his fear intensify. Anybody could have seen him being washed up just now. He shuffled along, not knowing where he was going. His clothes were torn and sodden. Every step left a muddy pool on the pavement, and his feet squelched inside his trainers.

Should he knock on one of these doors and ask to go to the police?

Then he heard two words in his head: *Neptune's Shadow*. They hummed in his ears beneath the sounds of the seagulls. He couldn't get rid of that voice. It was the scream of a dying man and it taunted him.

There was no way to ignore it. Jimmy could remember Bligh's words perfectly: *If we go down... Whoever survives...* Jimmy saw the image of the man flailing in the wind. It haunted him, but he forced himself to focus. *Take this information back to Colonel Keays. He has to know. He has to stop them.*

Outside the British Government, Jimmy was the only person in the world who knew that Neptune's

Shadow wasn't an oil rig, but a secret missile base, with rockets trained on Paris.

Suddenly, Jimmy felt like he was back in the plane, with the massive G-force holding him down. How much time did he have? Maybe he was too late already. How long had he been stranded on the ocean? His gut was in knots. For all he knew Paris had already been destroyed by British firepower, with thousands of people dead.

Jimmy shuddered and staggered to the side. It took a huge effort just to keep walking down the street. But where should he go? How could he get a message to Colonel Keays? And what would he say? He stopped and held his face in his hands, trying to force up those images he'd seen flash before him on the plane's display station – the aerial photographs of Neptune's Shadow. He had to remember. They only survived in his head.

His programming seemed to buzz in his head. One by one, Jimmy started to see lines forming. He could remember. Despite only seeing the images for a fraction of a second, it might be enough. If he concentrated, he could piece parts of them together. They were taking shape now.

Then he saw a flash of blue. Jimmy looked up. He swivelled to take in everything around him. There it was – a muddy white saloon car with POLICE in massive letters across the side and a flashing blue light on the roof. Jimmy froze.

"Well, hello there, amigo," drawled a lanky police

officer, stepping out of the driver's seat. "Welcome to Texas." His accent was a thick Southern American. His uniform was dark blue, with a badge on his chest, and hanging off his middle was a belt stacked with every piece of hardware he might possibly need.

Very slowly, his partner climbed out of the passenger seat – a fat man with no hair and a cruel smile all over his face. In his hands was a long, slim rifle.

"We're your ride back to Mexico," he said.

08 HAPPY RETURNS

"I haven't come from Mexico," Jimmy said in a hurry. "I've come from New York. I'm..." He was about to say that he was British, but stopped himself. He didn't want to say anything that could possibly attract NJ7's attention later if it was reported. He quickly put on an American accent – imitating it almost perfectly. "It's urgent that I speak to Colonel Keays or somebody in the CIA."

The two policemen shared a glance. The taller one sighed.

"Sorry, my friend," he said. "Your little American adventure is over. US Coastguard saw you washed up and radioed us." Step by step he edged towards Jimmy. "To be honest, they thought you'd be dead. See, we don't usually get 'em alive so far up the coast as this." He lifted some handcuffs off his belt and held them out in front of him. Jimmy's heart was pumping, but his eyes remained steady, taking in every movement.

"Don't make this mistake," Jimmy insisted, keeping his voice low and calm. "Do I look like I've come from Mexico?"

The two officers glanced at each other again. Jimmy couldn't tell what they were thinking. For a second he doubted himself. Maybe he did look like he'd been trying to smuggle his way into America across the Gulf of Mexico. Thousands of people tried it every year – but obviously most of them didn't make it this far alive.

"Look," said Jimmy, "all you have to do is make one call and you'll get this cleared up. Radio whoever you have to. Ask anyone in the Secret Service about a plane that went down." He held up his hands to try and calm the situation.

"A plane?" mumbled the officer with the rifle. "I didn't hear about any plane."

"Well, there was one," said Jimmy. "We crashed."

"When?"

"I don't know. I don't know what day it is."

"It's April 4th."

Jimmy froze.

"April 4th?"

"That's right. When did this plane of yours go down?"

Jimmy didn't answer. He wasn't listening any more. All he could hear was the date repeating over and over in his head. Then at last it sank in. *It's my birthday*, he thought.

He was suddenly aware of his fists clenching by his sides and his eyes watering. He took a deep breath, trying to clear his head. He could only think one thing. *It's my birthday.* The idea was so ridiculous it almost made him laugh, but at the same time it was tearing at his heart.

Then he saw the scowls on the faces of the two officers. Jimmy had paused too long. There was no way he was going to talk his way out of this now. The lanky man stepped towards him, brandishing the cuffs.

Should he give himself up? For a second Jimmy wanted to. But then he immediately dismissed it. If he let himself get arrested there was too much risk that he could be identified, even if the situation was cleared up later on. His face would be on camera at the police station. They might even take his fingerprints. And if the police had him on record it wouldn't be long before NJ7's electronic surveillance red-flagged the document for analysis.

No. He couldn't leave even the hint of a trail. To the British Secret Service, Jimmy Coates, the renegade assassin, was dead. And he had to stay that way.

"Turn round slowly," the policeman ordered, "and put your hands behind your back. You're coming with us."

Jimmy cautiously started following the instructions. Then, suddenly, he ducked to the right, putting the lanky officer between him and the other man's rifle. He rolled across the pavement, then leapt into the taller policeman's chest, leading with his shoulder. He connected with the force of an avalanche and felt the man's rib breaking on impact.

CRACK!

"Shoot!" the man yelled, the pain obvious in his voice. But Jimmy was too fast. He jumped up and landed on his back on the roof of the patrol car. He slid across the metal, his wet clothes greasing his way, and kicked out hard. He connected with the barrel of the rifle, sending it flying.

There was no way to stop Jimmy now. He tumbled to the ground on top of the fat man, then rolled off and hurtled across the street, diving into the alley between two houses. His muscles cried out inside him, and it wasn't just his face that was sunburned. His whole body was in agony. Within seconds he heard sirens. Already, his lungs were ready to implode, but Jimmy kept moving.

He twisted through the streets, his head down and his legs pumping. Every corner brought new sounds and new dangers. He listened for the direction of the sirens, but they seemed to be everywhere and closing in.

Every second that passed he could feel his body being drained of energy. The world was swirling around him. He was reeling from side to side. *Water. Food.* His body demanded it.

At last he saw a row of shops. One of them was a place selling tacky gifts. The store window was full of T-shirts, caps, mugs and novelty pencils, all emblazoned with 'Welcome to Port O'Connor'.

Jimmy dived in. The teenage girl behind the counter stood bolt upright in shock. Jimmy headed straight for a fridge stocked with drinks. On the bottom shelf were bottles of water. He tore open the fridge door and grabbed the largest one.

He knew he had no money on him, but there was nothing he could about it. It was stealing or dying. In one twist he unscrewed the lid of the bottle and took a swig. As the first gulp went down, he almost retched it straight back up again.

"Hey!" the girl shouted in a thick Texan accent. "This ain't a free bar, y'know?"

Jimmy ignored her and forced himself to drink more. There wasn't time to let his body recover slowly. Before the girl could draw breath to shout again, he grabbed another bottle of water and snatched a handful of chocolate bars from the rack, plus a packet of Mentos. Then he spun on his heels and burst out into the street. As he ran he poured water down his throat, not caring that it made his head dizzy and his stomach lurch.

Finally, he found an alley and collapsed in the shadow of a doorway, his chest heaving. His stomach retched violently and eventually he produced a spatter of vomit. He wiped his mouth on his sleeve and slumped against the building.

He tore open a chocolate bar. He had to force down every bite as quickly as he could – he had almost burned more energy than he had left. The milky texture felt so soothing on his tongue.

In no time Jimmy's heart rate was close to normal again. Even this small amount of water and food had done his body a huge amount of good. But it couldn't help his state of mind.

Neptune's Shadow. His finger scratched lines in the dust. He had to remember everything he had seen. He couldn't let the details fade. He knew that his programming made him capable of memorising incredibly complex images after only a second, but he wasn't in control of it. It was like having a camera built into his head, but not knowing how to turn it on.

Time after time Jimmy drew diagrams in the dirt. Were they accurate? He scrubbed them out and pounded his fist on the concrete. *Happy Birthday*, he thought sarcastically. With that, he pushed himself to his feet and started running again. He had to find a way out of town – a station, a boat, a bicycle even. Anything.

The one thing on his side was that there was hardly anybody about. He imagined that in the summer the town must be busy, but it was too early in the year for beach lovers.

With sirens still tearing at his ears, he wormed his

way through the town. At last he glimpsed the sleek silver body of a bus. The last passengers were climbing aboard, then the engine spluttered into life in a cloud of dust.

Jimmy dived to the ground. He rolled over three times, so quickly that at any one moment he couldn't tell whether he was facing the sky or the road. He caught the exhaust of the bus to stop himself abruptly. The fumes stung the roof of his mouth and the metal was growing hotter by the second, but Jimmy clung on. Eventually, he manoeuvred himself into a fairly stable position beneath the bus.

The noise and the heat drowned out the rest of the world. He was going to make it out of Port O'Connor. But Jimmy knew his struggle for survival was just beginning.

09 KOLAPORTID

Iceland's only flea market was Kolaportid, held every weekend in a vast warehouse on the harbour in Reykjavik. The sides of the building were open to the elements and the wind whipped in off the harbour, piercing Zafi's light fleece with ease. She was beginning to wish she'd actually bought that pink pashmina back in New York.

All around her were stalls selling everything in the world – bric-a-brac, antiques, clothes. Strange objects loomed out at every angle. The place was bustling and made to seem even more packed because everybody else was wrapped up in hefty Puffa jackets. All the men seemed to have thick beards as well, which must have helped in the cold. Zafi thrust her hands into her jeans and headed for a stand piled high with woolly hats.

Five minutes later she had some new woolly mittens and a bright red bobble hat. She was confident that the

French Secret Service budget would cover the cost. Now she headed for the food section. All she had to do was follow the smell.

At the back of the warehouse was a tiled extension. The stalls there were stacked with fish. Zafi was stunned by the selection on display. Some of the creatures looked like they should have died out with the dinosaurs. The floor was glazed with the muddy remnants of fish entrails. Her trainers slid about with each step, and every now and again she felt something squish.

Straightaway, she recognised the man she was looking for and approached his stand. He was fat, with round features, a neatly trimmed chestnut beard and glasses that made his eyes look too small for his face. Zafi stood on tiptoe and leaned forwards over the fish so that she didn't have to raise her voice too much above the noise of the market.

"You have a special order put aside for me," she said, looking her contact up and down.

"What name please?" the man asked, with a perfect English accent. Zafi paused for a moment to maximise the impact of her response.

"The Stovorskisson account." She loved the effect her words had on any of the contacts she used. The fishmonger's eyes stretched wide behind his glasses, like suns about to explode seen through a telescope. He wiped his hands on his overalls and stumbled back into a private room behind the counter. Every movement was stilted. Often these contacts were ordinary members of the public who had no idea of the extent of the operation they were involved with. Sometimes they didn't even believe they would ever really be called into action.

When the man returned he was clutching a small round container made of transparent plastic. In it were yellowish-white cubes that looked like some kind of cheese or fudge. They wobbled slightly as the fishmonger's hand trembled. He quickly put the container down on the counter, as if he didn't want to touch it any longer than he had to.

"You know," he said, almost too quietly to be heard, "the raw flesh of a Greenland shark is very poisonous."

Zafi tried hard to hide her smile.

"Of course," she replied. "It's the high concentration of trimethylamine oxide. To make it edible you need to bury it for six months to ensure thorough decomposition of the flesh, then dry it in a special shed for six more. The putrefied meat becomes *Hákarl*, an Icelandic speciality. In fact," she announced, a look of glee coming over her face, "I'll take a tub of that as well, please."

She picked up the plastic container the man had brought from the back and chose an identical one from a chiller.

"What are you going to do with it?" the man asked nervously, while Zafi counted out some money. "The raw meat, I mean?"

"Kill the British Prime Minister, of course!"

The man froze for a split-second, then his whole body relaxed. He reached over the counter and patted the bobble on Zafi's hat. A huge smile took over his face.

"Sweetheart, you've read too many science books," he chortled, then quickly added, "and too many spy books!"

Zafi flashed him her sweetest smile and waltzed away with her new weapon. The tubs of shark meat chilled her fingers. For a second, a thought flashed across her mind. *Do I have to do this?* She wondered what would happen if she dropped the tubs to the floor, letting the cubes scatter, and didn't stop to pick them up again. Immediately, her fingers locked more tightly around the plastic. *It's not up to me*, she told herself. *I can't change my blood.*

She wove in and out between the stalls, heading straight for the harbour.

BAM!

A massive weight smacked into her back, right at the top of her spine. There was a loud crack. She stumbled forwards, losing all control of her limbs for a second. She dropped her tubs of shark meat, showering the yellow cubes all over the floor. If it hadn't been for the fish slime on the soles of her trainers, she would have fallen. But instead she slid four metres, before finally catching her balance again. She spun round, her trainers giving a high squeak.

There was Mitchell. He'd swung down from the ceiling on an anchor rope. In fact, he was standing on one arm of the anchor. The other arm had Zafi's blood on it. Mitchell hopped to the ground and charged.

Zafi was reeling from the blow to the back of her neck. She could hardly see straight, but she could make out enough through the blur to know it was Mitchell. How had he tracked her? She thought she'd left him bamboozled in New York.

As for Mitchell, he'd come here to finish this cat-and-mouse chase with a single blow. But Zafi hadn't fallen. Her slide had saved her – for now. Mitchell plunged towards her, fists clenched above his head.

Just in time, Zafi dodged. She took shelter under a stall, but Mitchell threw himself on top of it. It snapped in the middle like a fresh cracker. Bric-a-brac hailed everywhere. A few of the shoppers around them screamed. The rest were too slow to know what was going on. One even asked the stallholder how much Mitchell's anchor was.

This was no cat-and-mouse chase. It never had been. These were two warring tigers.

Mitchell stayed there, lying on top of the broken stall. "You're trapped, Zafi!" he snarled. "There's nothing you can do."

Then, with the force of Iceland's biggest geysers, Zafi burst upwards, hurling Mitchell into the air. She ran for the exit, but Mitchell landed in a crouch, stretched his leg out and swept it round 360 degrees at amazing speed. It just caught Zafi's ankle. She tumbled forwards, but steadied herself on the anchor rope that was still hanging from the ceiling.

Before Mitchell could pounce on her again, Zafi seized the rope and swung the anchor round her head. Her arms looked too thin to lift such a weight, let alone hurl it around, but there was a deeper power fortifying her muscles.

Mitchell couldn't get close to her. Zafi swung the anchor faster, like poi twirling, gaining more control. It created a defensive shield around her. Mitchell grabbed at items from the stall and propelled them towards Zafi at different angles. First came an antique clock, then a pile of books, then an old sheep's skull that shattered into a thousand pieces when Zafi smashed it with the anchor.

It looked like the strangest game of baseball Iceland had ever seen, with every pitch a fierce fastball and every swing a home run.

But Mitchell wasn't here to play games.

"Give up," he bellowed. "I'm older – more developed.

More powerful. It's just a matter of time."

He bent forward, his weight spread evenly, and ran straight at Zafi. At the last second he took a false step to the left – a perfect dummy. Zafi's swing with the anchor was off the mark. Mitchell saw it coming as if the air was made of wax, slowing down everything that tried to pass through it. Everything except Mitchell.

He deliberately put his body in the way of the huge metal hook and caught it in his arms. Now he could use the impetus of Zafi's own swing against her. He swivelled and aimed high – one more kick to the back of the head and he could finish her.

But Zafi saw Mitchell coming. She pulled on the rope.

"Do you want power?" she whispered, lifting herself off the ground and performing a complete flip. "Or control?" She landed running. Mitchell's foot connected with nothing but the air. He turned in time to see Zafi's shadow disappearing into the harbour.

He let out a growl of frustration and kicked at the shark meat on the floor. He didn't care that the whole market was looking at him or that the wail of sirens filled the hall.

"Zafi!" he roared. "I'll never stop!"

Then he stormed off in the direction of the city centre.

10 SHADOW IN THE CROWD

Jimmy rolled out from underneath the bus as soon as it reached somewhere that seemed reasonably built up. The trip had taken several hours. His hands were raw, the muscles in his back ached and he felt like his insides had been carpeted in soot. He was in Bay City, Texas – but he wasn't staying. Within minutes he was at the train station, slipping through the ticket checkpoint, hidden in the crowd.

He stepped on to a train and moved through the carriages, not caring where it was going. When he reached the catering car he snatched up a trash bag waiting to be taken off the train. Not even knowing why, he untied it, reached in and pulled out a thick handful of used coffee grounds. He threw the rest of the bag out of the window just as the train lurched into motion.

The smell of coffee tormented him – he'd never known such hunger and thirst. He had barely replenished his energy enough to still be alive. He thought his stomach was going to suck his whole body into itself until he was just a quivering pink ball rolling about on the floor. He almost chuckled at that thought.

At the end of the next carriage Jimmy found the cleaning cart. He felt his programming fizz inside him. Jimmy distracted the cleaner by pretending to nod to somebody out of the window. He swiped a bottle from the trolley and ducked into a toilet cubicle.

He locked the door behind him and stared into the mirror. He hardly recognised himself. His skin was a nasty mixture of red and dark brown, with black corners where it was peeling – and it was peeling all over his face. His hair was matted and crusty with salt, just like his clothes. His arms and face were covered in grime from being under the bus and everything about him still stank of the sea.

He looked down at his fistful of coffee and the one-litre bottle of bleach. Time to transform his appearance. His breathing was slow, keeping his body artificially calm as he clogged the sink with toilet paper and poured in the bleach.

A few minutes later he emerged from the bathroom. His clothes were dyed various shades of brown. His hair was tinted chestnut and no longer spiked, but smoothed down across his forehead. Even his complexion looked smoother after he'd dabbed his skin clean.

For a few minutes, he stood by an open window, letting the blast of air dry his clothes a little and dissipate the strange smell of coffee, bleach and soap. Then he moved on again, looking for something to eat and a place to rest.

Jimmy slumped on a bench with a hoodie covering his head. He bit into a stale pastry he'd picked up as he was getting off the train. It was dry and chewy, but he needed it.

Jimmy was tucked away in one corner of Market Square, Houston. He'd chosen this spot carefully. From here he could see anybody approaching him from a long way off. He'd also positioned an old Coke can next to him so that he could keep an eye on what was going on behind him in its reflection.

He had changed his appearance again, in case anybody had seen him swiping food and water at every opportunity. He'd found his top with some jeans and a threadbare T-shirt in a box outside a charity shop. On his chest was the faded logo of a band that had split up ages ago. He'd had to roll up the legs of his trousers and he smelled of mouldy vegetables, but he didn't mind. At least nobody would be keen to approach him.

He felt bad about stealing even these small items.

When his programming showed him the opportunity, he couldn't stop himself. The assassin took over and Jimmy seemed to lose all sense of what was right and wrong – he only knew what was necessary. It was a question of survival.

People bustled through the square, but nobody lingered. Jimmy had never felt more alone. He was surrounded by crowds, yet the most important thing in the world was for nobody to know he existed. He wished he was back out on the water. The waves could have consumed him at any second, and he'd come close to dying of thirst and sunstroke, but at least he'd been unconscious.

While he was awake his mind tortured him with the memory of the deaths in the sky. Two agents. Both killed, both trying to help Jimmy. And yet Jimmy had done nothing to help them when the time had come. His hands shook when he thought about it.

He could feel his abilities growing. He was grateful that they kept him alive – any normal boy would have gone straight to hospital after surviving a plane crash, then days at sea without sustenance. But at the same time, his skills shocked him – their strength, their complexity and their consequences.

He was totally confident that he'd be back to full strength before long. He'd been built to survive. *And built to kill*, he thought. Jimmy clenched his fist and dug his nails into his palm. *No*, he insisted, *I'm in control now*.

He shuddered and chased the thought out of his head with another bite of his breakfast. *I could disappear*, he thought. He'd already witnessed how easy it would be for him to fade into the background of any city in the world. He was constantly adapting to his environment. It was as if he was some kind of chameleon – impossible for ordinary law-enforcement to track down. If he decided to, he was sure he could make it seem as if Jimmy Coates had completely vanished off the planet. Gradually, the thought took hold.

It was what he wanted, wasn't it? NJ7 already thought he was dead. Better than that, when the CIA heard about the attack on the plane they would assume that he was dead too. That would leave no possible way for Miss Bennett, or anyone in the British Government, to suspect that Jimmy Coates was still alive.

He looked across the square. With his skills, he knew he could move through the country like a ghost – not noticed and not bothered by anybody. Slowly, he would be able to build a new identity for himself. A whole life could be his. Not much of one, but a life free from the Secret Service, and free from the need for constant protection. The plane crash was his opportunity.

The muscles in Jimmy's legs twitched. They were urging him to stand up and take his place in the crowd as just another anonymous loner. Should he do it?

Jimmy thought of his family, concentrating on every line of their faces, every gesture that he could recall. If they believed he was really dead, it would devastate them. *But I could still vanish*, he thought, *and contact them later*. He pushed himself to his feet. His programming was ready to help him disappear.

But Jimmy held strong. He couldn't allow himself to do it. One thing was stopping him: Neptune's Shadow.

He had tried to find out whether Britain had already attacked France, but none of the newspapers seemed to say anything about it. Maybe that just meant it was already old news. Jimmy growled under his breath, trying to relax. *Come on*, he told himself. *Do nothing and NJ7 have won. You may as well be dead*. It was up to him tell Colonel Keays about Neptune's Shadow, whatever the risk. He had wasted too much time already.

He marched across the square to a public phone and snatched up the receiver. He could dial the operator. They could connect him to the Secret Service, or any branch of the Government. As soon as he mentioned Colonel Keays' name and the plane crash he'd be taken seriously.

Jimmy's finger paused over the number pad. It was like his hand had been encased in concrete and was too heavy to move. He couldn't dial. *They'll hear me*, he thought. He tried to reason with himself. There were billions of phone calls being made every day –

and thousands of people asking to talk to the CIA. At the same time, Jimmy knew that NJ7's electronic surveillance was second to none.

They'd already been able to hack into the US cellphone network in an attempt to jam Jimmy's programming. It was a matter of routine for them to have thousands of computers scanning the airwaves, recognising keywords, analysing every conversation, even processing voice patterns. They knew what was being said, and they knew who was saying it.

The second Jimmy breathed down that phone, a chain of electronic systems would be initiated that ended in a piece of paper landing on Miss Bennett's desk. She'd know he was alive and they'd come for him.

Jimmy stared at the receiver in his grasp. He could visualise the greasy prints forming beneath his fingers. It horrified him. NJ7 would track the call to that phone. They'd find his fingerprints. A shiver juddered through Jimmy's body. He couldn't touch anything. He couldn't speak. He couldn't be caught on camera. He couldn't look up in case the satellites recognised his face.

"I'm trapped," he whispered. "Trapped inside my own skin."

He slammed down the receiver. His eyes darted around the square. He was an animal, aware that any flicker could be the hunter who would end his life.

Finally, he pulled his sleeve over his hand and rubbed everything he had touched. Then he noticed a small LED window on the body of the phone. Jimmy stopped wiping and stared at the display. In small, grey digits it read,

5:54 – APRIL 4.

Jimmy slammed his fist into the phone. His knuckles crunched into the metal. He drew his hand back to punch again, but knew he was being stupid. The strength of his single punch had left a fist-sized dent in the body of the phone. The LED display was blank now.

Enough! he screamed at himself inside his head. *Forget that. You have no birthday. You have a mission. Get to New York.*

11 CITIZENS AGAIN

There was nothing extraordinary about flight BA719. It was a routine commercial flight from New York and, as usual, it was packed. There weren't many flights in and out of the UK these days because hardly anybody was allowed to visit. That meant tight competition for seats among the few businessmen who were still allowed to come and go.

Helen Coates led Georgie and Felix into the UK immigration hall. There was a huge queue – a snake of shuffling people, their heads downcast.

"Why do this many people want to come to Britain?" Georgie asked.

"Maybe all of their parents have been taken by NJ7 as well," Felix muttered. "Maybe it's the Government's cunning plan to try and increase tourism."

Georgie smiled, but her heart was twisting in her chest. She knew the pain Felix must be in and yet he never complained. He even managed to smile and crack his usual stupid jokes. *Maybe that's his way of dealing with it*, she thought. Then her mother put a hand on her shoulder.

"Remember what we talked about?" Helen whispered. "We're devastated about Jimmy. But don't overdo it. OK, here they come."

She gave Georgie and Felix a reassuring glance. Then Georgie turned to see Miss Bennett striding towards them on the other side of a glass partition. She was flanked by tall, muscled men in black suits. Each one bore a small green stripe on his lapel. Miss Bennett exuded power with every step. It was in the proud poise of her shoulders and the way she swayed from her hips.

Georgie could easily imagine her as a school-teacher. Even now, Miss Bennett was issuing a constant stream of instructions. Then Georgie noticed exactly who the instructions were aimed at and gasped. Her skin prickled with a mixture of excitement and anxiety. Marching behind Miss Bennett, struggling to keep up and frantically making notes on a palmtop computer, was Georgie's best friend Eva Doren.

Georgie stared. Her friend hadn't noticed her yet. What was she meant to do now? Had Miss Bennett brought her along deliberately, as some kind of test? As far as Miss Bennett knew, Eva had betrayed Jimmy and his family to go and work for NJ7. Georgie tried to work out how she'd react to seeing Eva if that had really been true. Was she meant to shout at Eva? Ignore her?

There was no time to decide. One of the agents with Miss Bennett opened a door in the glass and let his boss through.

"Welcome back," Miss Bennett announced, without a smile.

"A personal welcome!" Helen replied. "I thought you'd be busy lying, torturing and persecuting innocent people."

Miss Bennett's lips curled into a smug grin. She looked at Georgie. "Your mother and I are going to get on very well," she said, "if she keeps her mouth shut. Permanently."

Georgie put all her effort into keeping completely still and returning Miss Bennett's stare. In the corner of her eye, she could make out Eva. *Don't give anything away*, Georgie commanded herself.

"Leave her alone," Helen insisted. "Leave us all alone. Please. I've lost my son. Let me be a good mother to my daughter." She put her arm round Georgie's shoulders and gave a squeeze. It gave Georgie a warm feeling despite the coldness of the situation.

"You'll be watched," Miss Bennett announced. "Every second of every day."

"You'll get bored watching," Helen replied. "We won't be doing anything."

"I hope so." Miss Bennett looked Helen Coates up and down. "I promised Colonel Keays you wouldn't be killed. The second you do anything remotely interesting, I'm breaking that promise."

Now, for the first time, Georgie allowed herself to look directly at Eva. Her friend seemed relaxed – as if this was just another day at her work-experience placement. She even moved comfortably in the black business suit she had on. She was a miniature version of Miss Bennett – right down to the make-up. Georgie was horrified.

She desperately tried to catch her friend's eye, but Eva wasn't co-operating. She was either tapping her plastic stylus on the screen of her palmtop or staring straight ahead at the back of Miss Bennett's jacket. *What's happened?* Georgie thought. *Is she one of them now?*

Despair twisted her stomach. Then she forced herself to come to her senses. *Of course Eva's still on our side*, she thought. *How could I doubt my best friend?* She looked away and tried to concentrate on the conversation.

Miss Bennett turned to Felix. "What happened to your parents?" she asked. "Keays said something about them going missing in New York." Then she chuckled and added, as if it was a joke, "Did you lose them?"

Felix looked up at Helen, his mouth hanging open.

Georgie was sickened. She wanted to slap Miss Bennett in the face or, even better, kick her in the knee. Why was she taunting Felix like that?

"But you..." Helen stopped herself and took a deep breath. "We were separated from Neil and Olivia. I'm going to look after Felix."

"Lucky Felix," Miss Bennett nodded at last. "OK, he can live with you until we find some state-approved foster parents. Now come with me." She ushered them through the glass partition, into the area away from the rest of the crowd, and led them down the corridor in single file. The two NJ7 agents walked at either end of the line so there was no choice but to follow. "I assume you have no passports with you?"

They all shook their heads.

"Not to worry," Miss Bennett sighed. "My assistant will give you all the forms to fill in." She waved a hand in the direction of Eva, who was right behind her. Georgie had deliberately hung back so that they wouldn't be walking near each other. It was too risky.

Miss Bennett carried on, "Then we'll take your fingerprints, a DNA sample, a voice sample, a retinal scan, a confession of all your anti-British activities, along with an apology and an oath of loyalty. Then I have a team from anti-terrorism waiting to search you. And then – congratulations! You'll be citizens of the Neo-democratic State of Great Britain again. It might take a while to find you a home, of course, but until then you'll be in a State holding facility."

"Find us a home?" Helen asked. "What happened to the home we had?"

"That belongs to the Government now. Or the Prime Minister, should he ever need it again."

Helen was speechless. "You can't..." she choked on her own words.

Miss Bennett just marched on, not even dropping her pace. "Of course we can," she muttered. "Property is nationalised all the time." She looked up at Helen and dropped her voice. "By the way," she added hesitantly, "I'm sorry for your loss. I don't have any children, but I hope you can accept my sympathy and understand that it had to be done." She looked away, out of the floor-to-ceiling window at the grey world of the runway, and the planes' tail wings lined up like tombstones. "It was for the good of the country."

As they all walked on, Georgie started gently crying, without even really knowing why.

12 MOVIE NIGHT

It took two days for Jimmy to reach New York. Without any money and trying to keep out of sight of the police, he changed modes of transport at every opportunity: he'd been on trains, buses and boats. And he must have walked at least thirty kilometres as well. He'd had to keep moving. At times that meant not taking the most direct route, but at last he had made it.

He shuffled cautiously along 42nd Street, itching at the collar of a thick woollen shirt that he'd taken out of somebody's suitcase on a train. His trainers had come from the lost property desk at a bus station, along with the baseball cap that was pulled down low over his face. He had changed his appearance almost every hour, but he'd deliberately taken shoes that were a size too small to remind himself that he shouldn't be comfortable in clothes that weren't his.

The dazzling lights of Times Square made him blink

faster and he quickened his step. He bristled at having so many people around that could see him as if it was broad daylight. But he didn't have a choice. This was the place where he hoped to make contact with Colonel Keays.

Jimmy remembered his first encounter with the colonel. They'd met on the other side of a door that looked out of use, off a tunnel in Times Square subway station. It was the back entrance to what had once been the Knickerbocker Hotel. The hotel had closed down decades ago, and most of the building had been converted into a cinema. The CIA had taken the opportunity to create a hidden operations room.

But without any money, Jimmy couldn't enter the subway. The last thing he wanted was the New York Transit Police trying to arrest him for sneaking in without a ticket, just when he had come so close to his destination. So he hurried past the entrance to the station, knowing exactly what to try instead.

From the point where he was standing, he could see three different cinemas. One of them had to be the old Knickerbocker building. If Jimmy worked out which was the right one, he could find another way to the CIA ops room.

The crowd was getting denser and noisier. Jimmy's instincts kept him on high alert. His head snapped round every time somebody brushed against him.

He reached the AMC cinema on 42nd Street, just a few metres from Times Square itself, and pretended to study the movie times. Actually, he had spotted something far more interesting.

Next to the entrance of the cinema was a small area of the street that had been marked off with temporary barriers. A group of six workmen, all dressed in fluorescent yellow overalls and hard hats, were huddled around, clutching steaming mugs.

What work are they doing? Jimmy wondered. There didn't seem to be much for them to do and the pile of wooden planks at their feet had no apparent purpose. That was it – their feet. Three of the workmen had solid brown boots on – perfect for construction work. But three of them, who were otherwise dressed exactly the same as the rest, were wearing shiny black brogues more suited to office work – or the Secret Service.

Jimmy edged closer. The workmen were standing around an open manhole. Now Jimmy was sure that this was his way in. But could he just walk up to the workmen and ask? Jimmy didn't see that he had a choice.

He took a deep breath and drew on that strength that lay deep inside. He could feel it stirring in his veins. If for some reason he had made a mistake, he might have to make a rapid disappearance. He didn't want his programming to be far from the surface.

"I need to speak to Colonel Keays," he said quietly, trying to make sure only the workmen could hear him. They all towered above him. Their arms and shoulders bulged at the seams of their overalls. *Maybe they are construction workers after all*, Jimmy thought to himself.

One of them, with a round face and short beard, gave a shifty look out of the corner of his eye. "Get out of here, kid," he rasped. "We're busy."

Jimmy dropped his eyes to the man's polished shoes. He didn't want a confrontation, but he needed to make it clear who he was. "It's OK," he said calmly. "I know who you are. I need to get in to Knickerbocker to see Colonel Keays."

There was a moment's pause. The workmen glanced around at each other. Then suddenly the bearded man reached into his overalls and pulled out a Sig Sauer P229 pistol.

Adrenaline went fizzing through Jimmy's body. He barrelled into the temporary railing with his shoulder. It clattered into the agent with the gun, who rocked backwards. That moment, the other workmen reached into their overalls. Suddenly, Jimmy was facing six .357 calibre handguns. He froze, but the panic in his brain hardly registered with his body.

His programming had been working just to keep him alive. Now the predator was restless. It wanted to be let off its leash. Attack was Jimmy's job. He could feel it. These agents, like fools, had given him the chance to let rip and now he couldn't hold back. His strength had been gradually returning since the plane crash, and with it came the monster inside him.

Come on, he urged himself. He swallowed and closed his eyes, begging his body to stay calm. Slowly, he was able to raise his hands in the air. "Take me to Colonel Keays," he insisted, his voice wavering.

Now for the first time Jimmy heard screams – some people in the crowd had spotted the guns. Jimmy cursed himself for attracting attention.

"Get him off the street!" yelled a gruff voice. Someone grabbed him from behind in a concrete-hard grip. Jimmy forced himself to offer no resistance. Then whoever was holding him jumped down the manhole. Jimmy plunged into the dark.

"Get NYPD here to calm the crowd," a voice echoed down to him. "Tell them we were shooting a movie."

The workman landed on his feet, still clutching Jimmy, and grunted with the impact. Then he threw Jimmy to the ground in front of him. Jimmy's bones jarred on impact. He tensed his neck just in time to stop his head smashing against the stone floor.

"Taskforce Groundling!" the man bellowed into a small walkie-talkie device hidden inside his overalls. Then somebody from the street dropped a gun down the shaft. The agent caught it calmly and levelled the barrel at Jimmy's head. There was nowhere for Jimmy to go. The tunnel was too narrow to roll to the side.

"I have the assailant," the man announced. "Repeat: I'm pointing my gun at Mitchell Glenthorne. Do I take the shot?"

Jimmy gasped. "I'm not Mitchell!" he shouted as fast as he could. "I'm Jimmy! Jimmy Coates!"

The agent flinched, but his gun was completely steady in his hands. "Jimmy?" he said. "But you..." He stopped himself and flicked his eyes up to the street. "Secure the position!" he ordered, then looked again at Jimmy. "Jimmy Coa—?" he cut himself off in the middle of the word.

Jimmy nodded. The man lifted his foot. Jimmy thought he was about to get kicked in the face, but instead the man nudged Jimmy's cap off his face.

"Dammit!" the agent shouted. "You idiot!"

"What did I do?" Jimmy protested.

"Don't ever say your real name again! What if somebody up there had heard you? You're dead, remember?"

"What was I meant to do?" Jimmy yelled back. His cheeks burned with anger. "I had to tell you who I was – you thought I was Mitchell!"

"Yeah, well, what do you expect? There are only three child assassins in the world. Only two of them are male, and one of them – the only one who's on our side, by the way – was killed in a plane crash over the Gulf of Mexico." He tilted his head and glared. "Anyway, you had that cap pulled down over your face. And you English kids all look the same..."

"Are you going to put that gun away," Jimmy asked in a growl, "or do I have to put it away for you?"

The man hesitated for a second, as if he didn't want to be ordered around by a kid, but then his face relaxed. "It's good to see you, Jimmy," he mumbled. "But what the hell are you doing here?"

"I think I'd better explain that to Colonel Keays."

"Huh," the agent gave a sarcastic grunt. "Y'think?"

13 HOW TO CONTROL A COUNTRY

"Why didn't you just go to the police in Texas?" Colonel Keays barked. "Or any of the other States between there and here? And have you forgotten how to use a telephone? Or do you enjoy making a grand entrance?"

"I told you," Jimmy replied, trying to hold back his frustration. "In Texas they tried to arrest me and I didn't use the phone because NJ7'd flag up any call connecting to the Secret Service – even if I disguised my voice."

Jimmy was sitting at the bottom of the staircase in the defunct lobby of the Knickerbocker hotel, where he'd waited over three hours for Colonel Keays to arrive. Jimmy recognised the smell of the dust in the air. The windows were boarded up and well insulated, so there was no noise or light from outside. Only the hundreds of flickering bulbs in an ornate chandelier lit the room. The walls were blood red and covered in grime.

"I didn't realise your programming made you paranoid," said Colonel Keays.

"You'd be paranoid too if your country's Secret Service was trying to kill you."

"Well, fortunately, I *am* my country's Secret Service. I guess I can sleep easy. Ha!"

Jimmy couldn't help snarling. He'd been expecting gratitude. After all, Jimmy had struggled for days to make it back to New York and now he'd been able to pass on the vital intelligence from Keays' own agent. But instead, Jimmy was getting flippant remarks and a dressing-down. It felt like being in detention at school.

"So," he mumbled, "what are you going to do about Neptune's Shadow?"

Colonel Keays shook his head and dropped his gaze to the stains on the carpet. "Two good men," he said in the most sombre of tones. "I had concerns about that flight." He clenched his fist and squeezed his eyes shut. "I should have trusted my first instinct." He opened his eyes again. "We assumed you'd gone down with the plane as well, you know?"

Jimmy nodded. "Yeah," he said. "I thought you would have."

"I wish you'd…" Keays stopped himself. "Oh, what's the use now? It's good to see you're OK, that's all." He eased himself down with a sigh to sit next to Jimmy on the bottom step. It was one of the few moments when

Jimmy noticed Keays' age. He was sixty at least, but moved with such power and strength that he could have been much younger. It was usually only the medals on his uniform that showed his experience.

"You look thinner," he said.

"Been on a diet," quipped Jimmy.

Keays shrugged then said, in a matter-of-fact voice, "The information you've brought me, if it's true, is devastating. If Neptune's Shadow isn't really an oil rig, but a missile base, and if it has weapons trained on France in preparation for an imminent attack..." He paused and stroked his cheeks in thought. "Why would they sacrifice an oil rig?" he whispered to himself. "They're crazy."

"Why are they crazy?" asked Jimmy. "It kind of makes sense to me." He couldn't believe he was taking the side of the British Government, but it seemed like there was something Keays hadn't explained to him. "If I had missiles and wanted to point them at France, I think I'd probably hide them out at sea."

The colonel nodded. "You're right," he admitted. "But it's still a bad sign. It means Ian Coates is prioritising war over the economy."

Jimmy's face was blank.

"Look," Keays explained, "the old Prime Minister Ares Hollingdale was obsessed with everything in Britain being British. So he stopped the UK from importing almost all foreign goods, and that meant other countries decided to stop buying things from Britain."

"Yeah," I know all that," Jimmy cut in. "I lived there, remember?" He hated Keays talking to him like he was a baby.

"Ha!" Keays grinned. "Sure, sure, I forgot you know everything, Jimmy Coates."

Jimmy dropped his head, slightly embarrassed about his sarcasm.

"So the whole country could have gone bankrupt," Keays continued. "But Hollingdale had a plan. About eight years ago he sent in the army to seize the assets of the energy companies. He called it 'nationalisation', but to the rest of the world it looked a lot like stealing."

"He stole from companies? Like, their money?"

"Better than that. He took control of every oil field in UK waters – and there was nothing anybody could do about it. The world needs oil, Jimmy. No matter how much we try to live without petrol and plastic, we just can't seem to quit our old habits. Now, there isn't a huge amount of oil in the North Sea – it's nothing more than a dribble compared to what's in the Middle East – but there's enough. Even a small amount of oil is worth billions of dollars."

"But... but," Jimmy stuttered, "how can they...?"

"Get used to it, kid. It's happened before in other

countries and it will probably happen again. When you control the oil, Jimmy, you have the power and the money to control a nation."

"And now they've turned an oil rig into a missile base?" Jimmy was beginning to understand that the situation was even worse than he'd imagined. It looked like the UK was throwing everything they had into a war.

Keays shook his head in disbelief. "I'm glad you were able to get the information to me as quickly as you have," he said "But there isn't a lot the USA can do to interfere in affairs between the UK and France. We certainly can't send in forces. It will have to be diplomatic action and behind the scenes. I'll get on to the Ambassador in London."

There was something in Keays' voice that didn't sound reassuring.

"Do you think the Ambassador will be able to stop it?" Jimmy asked.

"I don't give him a chance in a million."

Jimmy was stunned by the colonel's certainty.

"So...so..." Jimmy stammered, "you mean there's no way of stopping Britain firing missiles at France?"

"If the British Government wants to do something, they usually find a way of doing it. I'm afraid negotiation and diplomacy just don't work with them any more. I thought things were going to change – President Grogan said he wouldn't support Britain in a war, and with your father in charge of Britain..."

"He's not my father," Jimmy snapped.

"Oh yes, of course. I'm sorry." Keays shook his head. "With Ian Coates in charge, I mean – I thought things would improve, but they seem to be getting worse."

"So what will happen if the missile strike goes ahead?" Jimmy asked, dreading the answer.

"France will strike back." Keays sounded so casual about it, as if he was predicting the weather. "There'll be casualties. On both sides."

"Can't we just warn the French Government?"

"We could, but that wouldn't stop the British attacking and it might just make France more ready to retaliate." He took a long look at Jimmy. "I'm afraid now isn't a good time to be in Paris or London."

Jimmy felt a rush of horror coursing through his guts.

"Where's my mum?" he rasped. "Where's Georgie?"

14 IT CAN BE DONE

Jimmy stared into Colonel Keays' eyes, searching for any sign of what he feared most. But the colonel's face didn't flicker.

"Tell me they're safe," Jimmy begged. "Tell me you hid them somewhere in America. Or anywhere else in the world."

"I sent them back to the UK," Keays explained slowly. "With you safe, there was no reason to keep them here, and your mum wanted to look for Felix's parents."

"Look for his parents?" Jimmy's fear was taken over by confusion.

Keays nodded and let out a deep sigh. "I'm sorry, Jimmy, I should have told you, but there were so many other things we needed to talk about."

"You should have told me what?" Jimmy tried to keep his voice level, but he was hardly able to control himself.

"While you were escaping New York, Neil and Olivia Muzbeke were taken from the safehouse. We think NJ7 has them."

Jimmy couldn't believe it. One disaster was piling on top of another. He felt like even the walls of the building would crash in on him at any second. He held his head in his hands. In the darkest corner of his mind, he was aware of vague shadows playing out scenes. His programming was already planning a violent attack on Britain in his imagination.

"We've got to get them out," he whispered. "They'll all be killed. If NJ7 doesn't do it, the French will with their missiles when they retaliate." He paused for a second. "And why shouldn't they strike back?!" he shouted. "If Britain attacks them for no reason? It's crazy!"

Jimmy couldn't sit still. He jumped up and paced the room, clenching and unclenching his fists. "He's got to be stopped. That man can't just start a war because he feels like it."

"I think it's more complicated than that, Jimmy."

"But why?!" Jimmy screamed. "It doesn't need to be, does it? If he attacks France, thousands of people will die – or millions! And that's going to include Mum and Felix and Georgie…" He could feel his face creasing up, but he refused to give in to the tears. He was too angry to let go of the emotion. "I thought everyone was going to be safe," he whispered. "I thought it was over."

"I know," said Keays. "So did I."

Jimmy couldn't speak any more.

"Here," said Keays gently, reaching into his jacket. Then he held out a page of notepaper folded neatly in half. Jimmy half turned away, watching out of the corner of his eye. "It was your birthday recently, wasn't it?" Jimmy nodded reluctantly. It was the last thing he wanted to be reminded about. "Your sister and your friend wrote you a birthday message before they left."

It was a few seconds before Jimmy gathered the courage to take the paper and open it. As soon as he did, the corners of his mouth twisted downwards and he had to wipe tears from his eyes.

He recognised his sister's neat and loopy handwriting immediately. She'd filled most of the paper. Jimmy read through it as fast as he could, worried that if he lingered over it, he wouldn't be able to get through to the end without breaking down. Her message said:

Happy Birthday! Sorry u don't have a present from me. I'd get a book or something, but I don't know what ur favourite type is, but I know u know mine. We'd have to discuss it, For, um, like, ages. Anyway, really missing u already. But I

know I'll see u again. I promise. I'd put
everything on the line for it.
We'll be thinking for u.

Jimmy didn't even pause to think about what he'd read, because at the bottom was Felix's unmistakable scrawl. For some reason, his friend always liked to write in capitals, and Jimmy knew he was one of the only people in the world who could actually read it. The thought almost made him laugh.

Felix had written:

HAPPY BIRTHDAY! NOT MISSING u.
No WAY. IN FACT, WHo R u
AGAIN? ANYWAY, uR SISTER'S
GIVEN SoME GooD ADVICE So Do
WHAT SHE SAYS. CYA. BYE.

As soon as the words went through Jimmy's mind, he forced them out again. Even the feel of the paper in his hands threatened to overwhelm him, so he quickly shoved the note into his back pocket and pretended to be scratching his head.

"Look," said Keays, his deep voice rattling the chandelier, "I know you're worried. But you've already made your decision. It's amazing that you've convinced

Miss Bennett that you're dead. You can't go back to Britain now."

"I don't want to," Jimmy cut in. "I never want to see that place again. It's not my home any more."

As soon as he said it, Jimmy's chest tightened. Britain wasn't his home any more, but that's where all the people he cared about were.

"I'm pleased to hear you say that, Jimmy. Your family and your friends can live their lives now. You've saved them. And you can live a decent life too, once we relocate you."

Jimmy was hardly listening. He didn't want to be reassured. Anger and frustration churned inside him. They had been building up since the second he was shot down over the Gulf of Mexico.

"Fine," he announced suddenly. He could feel his heart toughening, strengthening his resolve. "But what about force?"

"What are you talking about?" Keays asked.

"You said negotiation wouldn't work. With the British Government. With my... with the Prime Minister and Miss Bennett."

"I'm afraid that's right. You see we've tried..."

"So what about force?" Jimmy interrupted. He held himself tall and squared his shoulders.

"Force?"

"Yeah. The Marines, the army or... whoever. It

doesn't matter. Somebody…" Jimmy's voice grew louder and in the background was the rumble of an explosion coming from one the movies showing above them. "Someone's got to be able to take out the British missiles at Neptune's Shadow."

"Look, Jimmy," Keays replied, holding his hands out and his palms up. "Sure, I mean, I could send in a unit of the Marines, and yeah, they could neutralise the base. Ha! They could take down any missile base in the world. Hell, I could flatten it in seconds with the push of a few buttons and a single surgical strike from an unmanned aircraft. If there's any oil there at all…" He made the shape of an explosion with his hands. "BOOM! The whole place will go up like 4th July." Jimmy stepped back, shocked at the hint of excitement in the colonel's eyes. "But it won't do any good, Jimmy. You know why?"

Jimmy knew exactly what Keays was going to say. He was ready for it, so he just dropped his head and let the man carry on with his speech.

"You couldn't do it in secret," said Keays, puffing out his chest as if he was showing off his medals. "It's an almost impossible task for anybody to penetrate the base, disarm it and make it out alive without being detected. I can't think of a way anybody could do that even in ideal conditions. We don't even have plans of the base, do we? You're the only source we have on this. All we've got is the inside of your head."

He reached out to ruffle Jimmy's hair, but Jimmy slapped his hand away and stepped back. Keays looked shocked and his voice became suddenly more serious.

"It can't be done, Jimmy," he declared. "Not without it being obvious that US forces did it. Then the UK wouldn't just be at war with France – they'd be at war with us too! And, you know what, Jimmy? Being at war with the US is a whole new ball game. It's not even the same ballpark. You think a scrap of London would be left standing? *Do* you?" Jimmy didn't move. He refused to give in to Keays' bullying. "You want to put your friends in that situation? You would just have made things a helluva lot worse."

Jimmy waited for the air to clear. The colonel's cheeks were red and he was slightly short of breath.

"It can be done in secret," Jimmy said softly.

"Don't be a fool, Jimmy Coates," the colonel said with a dismissive wave of his hand. "I didn't get these medals for nothing. I can mount any operation I want. But not this one – because it's impossible. And pointless." He turned away and pulled a slim mobile phone from his jacket. "I'm going to start making arrangements to put you back into hiding. For good this time."

Jimmy stayed completely calm. Then he said something that put a sly smile on Keays' face and made the man put away his phone.

"It is possible. I'll do it."

15 SYNPERCO

Jimmy's first glimpse of the *Risavottur* came from a helicopter a hundred metres up – and it took his breath away. It was by far the biggest ship he had ever seen: over three hundred metres long and sixty metres wide, but for an oil tanker that was only about average.

Jimmy leaned out of the helicopter to get a better view, squinting against the fierce wind of the North Atlantic. The sides of the ship rose out of the water like the walls of a fortress and were over thirty metres high. The lower half was painted red and the rest was solid black except for a grey circle right at the front with a fat black 'S' painted on it. It was a logo that gave Jimmy the sliver of a memory, but it quickly passed.

Crew strode all over the deck, in bright orange Puffa jackets and yellow sou'westers. After a moment, Jimmy realised that they were clearing a small area on deck in preparation for his arrival.

"Ready?" called out the pilot.

Jimmy gave a strong thumbs-up. Less than a minute later he was clambering down a rope ladder on to the deck of the *Risavottur*. As soon as his foot touched down, two crewmen wrapped him in a Puffa jacket just like their own and planted a sou'wester on his head. Jimmy couldn't help smiling. He felt like a member of the crew already. He gave a final signal to the helicopter, then the rope ladder was pulled up and the chopper was away.

Jimmy turned to see the broad smile of a very large man, whose bulbous crimson nose stuck out over the top of his layers of insulation. His cheeks were almost the same colour as his Puffa jacket and lined with veins.

"Welcome aboard!" he shouted. "I'm Captain Peck." His voice was thin and rough, with an accent that was hard to place with the noise of the wind and the fading rotors of the helicopter. To Jimmy it sounded half American and half Scandinavian, but the man's English was precise. "Get this boy some gloves!"

Jimmy hugged his beefy Puffa coat closer round his body. It was like a full-length suit of bright orange rubber rings. Nevertheless, Jimmy was freezing. He'd been on board less than an hour, and he was already wishing he'd been able to go all the way to Neptune's Shadow in the chopper. He knew that would have attracted attention, but the noise, the wind and the roll of the ship were too great for him to think straight. *Great design, NJ7*, he thought to himself. *A seasick assassin*.

He spat the salt-spray from his mouth and a stream of saliva blew straight back into his face. *Perfect*, he thought.

"Jimmy!" came a shout from the wheelhouse. With a sense of dread, Jimmy lumbered back across the deck. He knew that indoors, the overpowering smell of oil and the shifting of the sea would make him feel even more nauseous.

"Try some of this." Captain Peck thrust a mug of hot chocolate into Jimmy's fist.

Jimmy took it with a weak smile and slumped down on to an old wooden chair, clutching his stomach. The wind rattled the walls of the cabin. There was a big table filling the room that seemed to be shifting with the roll of the boat, but then Jimmy noticed it was actually nailed to the floor.

"Don't worry," said the captain. "I know how you feel. My first mission for the CIA involved a whaling expedition. Didn't see a single whale. I was too busy throwing up into a Wellington boot. But that was a long time ago now. You get used to it. These days I feel sick on land!"

Jimmy tried to laugh, but failed.

"Anyway," Peck went on, "Colonel Keays wanted me to reiterate: you don't have to do this."

"I know," said Jimmy, telling himself to ignore his sickness and get on with things.

"But if you do decide to go through with it, I need you to understand that you do so alone. OK?"

Jimmy nodded.

"OK," Peck repeated, thrusting a piece of paper and a pen into Jimmy's hands. "Then sign this."

"What's this?"

"A disclaimer. It says that if anything happens to you, the US military isn't responsible." Peck paused for a moment, then added, "It says that you won't sue us."

Jimmy couldn't believe it. He started reading through the contract, but halfway down the page, the words stopped going in. The contract had set Jimmy's mind racing with other thoughts.

Was he crazy? He was going in, alone, to disarm a secret British missile base. The US Secret Service couldn't offer him anything except a ride in case it caused an even worse international incident. If anybody recognised him or if his face was picked up on security camera, his family would be interrogated and killed. Then they'd come after him – that's if he was lucky enough to survive.

Jimmy gulped. He scribbled his name at the bottom of the piece of paper and shoved it back in Captain Peck's direction.

"We're taking you to the edge of the Arbroath oil field but no further, OK?" the captain announced. "Synperco has permission for passage through UK waters from Iceland to Holland, but we can't go too near Neptune's Shadow itself. So from the edge of the oil field you're on your own."

"Syn-what?" Jimmy asked.

"Synperco. It's a small US oil company. You're sitting on one of its tankers. We borrowed it so that nobody would have any suspicions about us sailing round the south coast of Iceland and past the Outer Hebrides. Then we turn south towards the North Sea oil fields, but you'll have to complete the journey on your own."

"You mean swim?"

Peck nodded. "Sure," he said casually. "We have diving equipment and everything, but Colonel Keays said you wouldn't need it."

Jimmy didn't answer. The thought of swimming still made him shudder. It was a reaction left over from the time before his powers came to the surface, when he would almost drown in a swimming pool, let alone breathe underwater in the North Sea.

"You neutralise the base," Peck went on, ignoring the fear in Jimmy's expression. "Do it without anybody knowing you've been there. I'll be waiting in Dutch waters on another ship. Here's the location and what it'll look like." He pulled out a brown folder from inside his coat and spread the files out on the table. Jimmy pulled himself up to have a look.

The folder contained a chart of the waters of Northern Europe with some co-ordinates marked just off the coast of Holland, and a photograph of another huge oil tanker, but a white one painted with the letters 'OPEC'.

"OPEC?" Jimmy asked.

"The Organisation of Petroleum Exporting Countries," Peck explained. "A neutral vessel. Or it's meant to be, anyway. Obviously, it isn't a real one, but nobody will question it. As soon as you reach us, I'll send in a small OPEC team to take control of the rig. It'll look like a routine check. Got that?"

Jimmy made a strong effort to implant the location marked on the map into his head, then pushed the papers aside. "Thanks, Captain," he said, trying to sound completely calm.

"Is that it?" Peck asked, looking confused.

"What?"

"You just look at these and that's all you need to know? Do you understand what you're taking on here?"

Captain Peck's disbelief was almost infectious, but Jimmy held himself together.

"This is a job that even a top marine unit couldn't pull off," the captain went on. "A whole team! You're going to be on your own. Forget about completing the mission – do you know the strength you're going to need just to swim there?"

Jimmy rested his head in his hands and still didn't say anything. His stomach was more queasy than ever. It wasn't just seasickness. How could he possibly do this? He didn't know what his plan was. He had been relying on his programming to come up with something while he was on the ship. He needed it to work for him, though he could feel it growing every minute. Controlling what it would do was becoming more and more of a fight – and he hadn't expected seasickness to get in the way.

But Jimmy was determined to close down the missile base, even if his assassin instincts resisted heading straight into danger. Even if it cost his life. He had to at least try. The consequences of giving up now were too disastrous to contemplate.

The captain ranted on, growing more and more agitated, his voice grating on Jimmy's nerves. "Shouldn't you be asking me about the details of the base?" the man insisted.

"Do you know them?" Jimmy was shocked.

"Of course not!" Peck yelled. "Nobody does! For all I know it might not even exist."

"So what do you want from me?" Jimmy shouted back, becoming more annoyed every second.

"Just tell me you have a plan. You seem like a good kid and frankly, Jimmy, I'm not interesting enough to be the last person you ever speak to."

Jimmy drew himself upright. There was something buzzing inside him, sending shivers through his entire skeleton. It calmed his nerves and forced him to breathe slowly and deeply.

"The swim will be easy," he whispered, surprised that he was even speaking. His voice was so soft it was almost drowned out by the drone of the ship's engines and the creak of the cabin. "That chart had the currents marked on it. I'll find the slipstream. It'll carry me straight to the rig."

In his head, details of the nautical chart flashed up even more clearly than what he could see in front of him with his eyes. And they didn't stop. Instead, they melded into something else. Jimmy's hands moved before he knew they were going to. He snatched Captain Peck's ballpoint pen just before it rolled off the table.

He cleared the dust from the surface and started scratching at the wood with the biro. After a second, Jimmy recognised what he was drawing – the layout of Neptune's Shadow. To his relief, the aerial photographs of the base were at last flooding out from his memory.

"Here," he announced, brushing away splinters and prodding the middle of the table. "In the central hall. That's the most likely place for the missiles to be stored." His voice came out with such authority and confidence that it almost scared him. "It's where a normal rig would have the principal oil receptacles. That's the only area with enough space, even on a rig this size. Once I've found them, I just have to sabotage the launch mechanism. That should be easy."

Now his hands carried on moving across the table, scratching more lines into the wood. Captain Peck was dumbfounded – and inside, Jimmy felt the same. He couldn't believe his control and precision with the pen, let alone the fact that his mind had managed to retain so much information. He'd only seen it for a split second on the display unit of the spy plane, just before the crash, but now his programming recalled it with ease.

"Then there's the control unit for the missiles," he went on. "That will be in the pump room. It has to be. That's where the computer systems would be most protected from external power surges." He stopped to catch his breath.

Captain Peck ran his hand across Jimmy's diagram. "You've scratched up my table," he said with a smile. "Don't the British use paper?"

Jimmy was hardly listening. "It's all in here," he whispered, looking over what he'd drawn, checking each line again and again. "It's inside my head. I'm made to do this. Seek and destroy."

"It's OK," Peck said, putting a hand on Jimmy's

shoulder. "You're doing it for the right reasons now."

Jimmy nodded. He knew Peck was right, but there was something nagging at the back of his mind. First, he thought it was fear for his mother and sister in London, unaware that if Jimmy failed they'd be blown to bits by the French. He had to put that to one side if he was to complete his task.

Still some doubt revolved in his head. He knew nothing about the security at the base. He had to be ready to handle anything the British threw at him. He had to be fully in command of his assassin's instinct. The thought made his throat tight and his stomach heavy.

Finally, he looked up at Captain Peck and ordered, "Get me a diving suit and a tin of tuna. When we reach the oil field, I'll be ready."

16 FEEDING THE FISH

The flowers in the pots round the front door had died, but they had always seemed to do that. Felix was surprised to see that the windows weren't all boarded up – only the one on the ground floor that was smashed. For a couple of minutes, he thought about breaking in. It wouldn't have been too difficult. He reckoned he could even have climbed the front of the house and tumbled straight into his own bed. But it wasn't his bed any more. It belonged to the State. *Just like my parents*, he thought.

He stayed on the other side of the road, looking the house over. *It's just a building*, he told himself. *I could build a better one myself if I had enough bricks.* His mind wandered off, picturing all of the places he could look for spare bricks and trying to work out roughly how many he'd need. *A million will do*, he thought.

"You OK?" said Georgie softly.

Felix jumped. He'd forgotten she was there. They'd come here together as a detour after school. NJ7 had moved Felix to Georgie's school. They hadn't had any choice about it. It was to make it easier to keep an eye on them. NJ7 were always watching. As if the surveillance cameras all over the school buildings weren't enough, there was always an NJ7 agent hovering around them.

It wasn't great for Felix's social life, to say the least. His friends from his old school, where he'd been with Jimmy, may as well not have existed any more. And new friends weren't really his top priority.

Felix shrugged and put on an over-the-top sad face. His lips curled downwards like a crazy clown. He knew he was meant to feel upset. After all, his parents had been secretly taken by the British Secret Service. But really he couldn't work out how he felt. That was partly why he'd wanted to come to his old house.

"Let's go," he said suddenly. "I'm cold."

They walked in silence back to their new home – a State-approved flat. A tall bald man in a black suit followed them all the way. He wasn't trying to conceal himself. Instead, he had a mobile phone pressed to the side of his head and talked in a low voice. On the back of the phone was a green stripe.

* * *

Jimmy squeezed into his diving suit. It was like a standard wetsuit but made of thicker rubber, with a hood that covered Jimmy's head. The CIA had managed to get hold of one in a junior size. It was actually slightly too small, but Jimmy made the best of it. It covered his feet, but unfortunately the gloves were too big and kept falling off, so Jimmy left them on the table.

For anybody else that would have been unthinkable, and they would have needed a drysuit rather than a wetsuit, to keep warm. But Jimmy was only after an extra layer of insulation as a boost to his natural defences while he was under the water. He didn't want to have to battle the cold at the same time as fighting the British Navy.

"They'll have cameras," Captain Peck said quickly. He pulled a black canvas bag from under the table. In it was a diving mask. "You'll need this. Look." He turned the mask around and Jimmy saw that it wasn't standard. Inside was a wire attachment that looked like a torture device.

"Oil rigs have cameras that operate heat-sensing, face-recognition software," the captain explained. "It means the cameras can see through masks and balaclavas and reconstruct the shape of an attacker's face."

"What?" said Jimmy, confused. "They don't have that anywhere on land. At least, not that I've seen."

"It was so they could build a database of

environmental campaigners and saboteurs. A US arms company just sold them all the kit."

"So what does this mask do?" Jimmy asked. "Apart from dig bits of wire into my face?" He examined the inside of the mask more closely. "And why does it have fake ears?"

"The software is designed to see past normal disguises – masks, beards, skin colour, things like that. So instead it looks for things that don't usually change – like the shape of your eyebrows and your ears."

Jimmy nodded and reluctantly pulled the mask over his head. It covered everything from his top lip upwards, leaving his mouth and chin free. The wires bit into his forehead, pulling his muscles in every direction except the one they were meant to go in. Jimmy caught his reflection in the windows of the wheelhouse. He was leaner than he used to be, though his shoulders seemed a little wider. Most noticeable were the false ears on the sides of his head.

"This is stupid," he mumbled. "I look like a clown."

"You'll have to speak up, Jimmy," Captain Peck sniggered. "Or Noddy won't hear you."

Jimmy couldn't believe he was going to have to disarm a missile base wearing a mask that stabbed him with wire prongs and fake rubber ears that made him look like Dumbo. It wasn't even his face that NJ7 would recognise.

"Got anything to make me look less like a twelve-year-old?"

Captain Peck stopped smiling. They both knew the limitations of what Jimmy was wearing. As soon as anybody saw a child on the base, they'd know who it was.

"Better not get spotted, I suppose," Peck shrugged.

Jimmy felt a lurch of terror in his chest. He was still queasy from the roll of the ship and every time he focused on what he was about to try to do, he thought he was going to throw up. It was only his programming that made him seem so calm.

"Hand me the tuna," he ordered.

"Hungry, Jimmy?" Peck asked, twisting the handle on a rusty tin opener to force it round the large can. "You shouldn't eat before you dive."

Jimmy ignored him and grabbed the tuna. It was with a strange pride that he smeared himself all over with the chunks of fish. *Did I think of this myself?* he wondered. He couldn't tell. It might have been just one more thing that his programming made him do automatically. Every day it was becoming harder to tell where his old self ended and the growing assassin began.

Within a few minutes, a team of crewmen was lowering Jimmy to the water on a small platform, rocked by the wind. They'd turned off the lights on the ship to give him the cover of almost total darkness. The moon was just a faint glow coming through the clouds and the spray of the sea reduced visibility even further.

Jimmy pushed himself off the platform. The water was cold at first, but he quickly adjusted and wearing the diving suit really helped.

The air seemed unnaturally quiet – there was only the wind and the patter of the rain falling on the water. Jimmy drifted into the darkness. When he looked round, the *Risavottur* was already gone. The surge of the sea lifted him over twenty metres, then plunged him down again. He felt like a twig bobbing along the surface.

Jimmy delved into his mind, marshalling his programming to drive him on. He had to get to Neptune's Shadow as quickly as possible. He gathered his strength and swam with the current. He'd estimated that with the water on his side, it would only take about an hour to reach the base. But now Jimmy realised what a task that was.

After nearly two hours, Jimmy felt like the muscles in his shoulders and chest would never work again. He gritted his teeth and doubled his effort. With no landmarks it was impossible to tell how much progress he was making. The thick mist on the North Sea refused to lift and Jimmy could only watch the shadows shifting in the water beneath him.

Then, just as he was starting to doubt whether he would ever find the missile base, something caught his eye. A light. Jimmy's skin tingled. The clouds were too thick for it to be a star and it was too low on the horizon to be a helicopter or plane.

The closer Jimmy got, the more that whole area of the sky was illuminated. The fog was coloured an amazing display of blues, reds and whites. Some lights flashed; others remained constant. Then suddenly the mist parted and what Jimmy saw was awesome.

A huge tower rose into the night sky, with flashing lights all the way up and a revolving beacon at the top. Jimmy had to strain his neck to look at it. He couldn't help gaping. He'd never seen an oil rig and this had been one of the largest in the world, before they converted it into a missile base. He never realised there were structures out at sea that were as massive as skyscrapers.

That wasn't all. The body of Neptune's Shadow looked like a god had come down and built a Lego city on the water. Blocks of scaffolding and metal platforms jutted out at extraordinary angles. Above them, cranes arched out of the rig like arms about to snatch the clouds.

This was it. Time to dive. He checked his mask was secure around his head and forced his body downwards into the water. Within seconds, all the light from the surface was gone. Jimmy had to rely on his night-vision to guide him, but the water was thick with black algae. He only saw what was less than a metre in front of him.

Then his breath ran out and his chest cramped for air. It was the moment he'd been dreading. Jimmy drew in a gulp of water. He thought his head was going to explode. The salt burned his throat and even crept up his sinuses to sting his eyes. He immediately felt like he wanted to throw up, but something inside him forced him to ignore the discomfort. He kept on swimming, hardly able to see. Twice he nearly swam straight into a school of fish and had to twist at the last second.

Jimmy had no idea what enabled him to breathe underwater. All he could feel was his diaphragm working harder to draw water into his lungs and the burn in his throat. Actually, the hundreds of tiny sacs in his lungs were inflating with water just as they would with air. They were surrounded by capillaries filled with blood, just like a normal human, but an extra filtration system pulled in the oxygen and converted the hydrogen into nitrogen hydride.

Diving towards the seabed was much harder than swimming on the surface had been. Jimmy was no longer simply pushing himself along with the current and he wasn't equipped with weights. The forces beneath the surface were weaker, but much more complex. It was also colder down here. The deeper he went, the harder his muscles had to work, and they were already operating at their limit. Then he started to notice the effects of the water pressure.

It felt like being sucked into a giant plastic bag and squeezed from all sides. A huge weight was pressing in on him. Every organ crumpled inside him and soon every bit of his body was screaming at him to give up – his lungs, his arms, his eyes. But he had no choice now. *Keep going*, he urged himself. *Get to the rig.*

He was over a hundred metres down when he finally got what he wanted. The fish smell from the tin of tuna hadn't been completely washed off him. It was still strong enough to attract the attention of a common skate.

Shaped like a stingray, but without the deadly poison, the skate flapped out of the darkness at him. Jimmy lurched out of the way, taken by surprise. But then he realised that his plan was working. For a few seconds he stopped kicking, not wanting to scare the skate away. Then it came again, attracted by the smell of dinner. It hovered down, looming over him. It was over two and half metres long, with a span that was easily enough to cover Jimmy.

Very carefully, Jimmy started kicking again. The skate stayed with him, stroking Jimmy's back with its wings. If he hadn't been so tense, Jimmy might have laughed. It was the strangest feeling, and a reassuring one. Jimmy knew that every centimetre of water in the area would be monitored by cameras, above and below the surface. Depth was no protection. But as long as the skate was covering him, Jimmy wouldn't be seen, and if he triggered any sensors, base security would call it a false alarm.

The water around him grew lighter with every stroke. Jimmy was approaching the legs of the base. It was a fixed platform rig, which meant the legs were rooted to the spot. It also meant Jimmy would be able to climb right into the heart of Neptune's Shadow.

17 NEPTUNE'S WELCOME

Jimmy's fingers were almost too cold to grip the metal. Even with the distorted colour of his night-vision he could tell that they were more purple than pink. But still, he shook off the skate and started his climb.

It was only now he had stopped swimming that he noticed the vibrations in the water. It was as if the whole sea was rumbling. Was that the missile launch? Was he too late? He quickened his pace, but kept slipping off the metal rigging and having to catch himself again. The blood wasn't returning to his fingers. He could make a fist, but his grip was weak.

As he climbed, the vibrations continued. They didn't get any stronger though. In fact, as Jimmy approached the surface, they were getting weaker. It couldn't be the launch of a missile, Jimmy knew that now. So what was it? He tried to peer through the water at the rest of the structure around him. The base was so large that he could barely make out the contours of the legs at the other three corners. To his right was the core of the rig and it was moving – the rig was still pumping up oil.

Jimmy's brain was working as hard as the rig. Why was the missile base still active as an oil rig? Maybe having one of the world's largest rigs not pumping any oil would be too conspicuous.

Jimmy rushed the last few metres and broke through into the air with a rush of gratitude that he was still alive. Straightaway, he choked up what felt like a whole river of water. He coughed so hard that he thought the lining of his throat would tear. His next couple of breaths were like stabs in the chest, but Jimmy loved the feel of the air going into his body again. He tried to wipe the slime away from his mouth, but the back of his sleeve just made it even slimier. Then a huge wave crashed over him.

The lights of the rig were blasting down on the whole area now, so for the first time in hours his night-vision faded away. But Jimmy's hands were still blue. In fact, the ends of his fingers had gone black.

Suddenly, he realised that he shouldn't have worn a diving suit. It had fooled his programming into thinking the water was warmer than it was which meant his circulation hadn't compensated. Now he was going to suffer for that mistake. The pain was incredible.

It throbbed from his hands all the way to his elbows. But even worse, he couldn't feel some of his fingers at all.

He looked up. Neptune's Shadow rose over him with all the might of the planet it was named after. He was nowhere near the platform of the base. There was still a long stretch of metal rigging to climb. Without the buoyancy of the water to support him, it felt like he was dragging metal weights on his ankles and the wetsuit limited how far he could stretch.

For the first part of the climb, waves smashed into him every few seconds. After that, the wind whipped around him, threatening to blow him right back into the water. Jimmy clung on, but it was anguish. He glanced upwards – halfway there. He felt so close now and put all his energy into every heave. Then he heard a noise that came like a stab in the heart.

"Do not move!" It was a man's voice over a loudspeaker.

Jimmy hadn't realised what a horrible feeling it would be to hear an English accent again. His breath quickened and a nasty shiver ripped through his body. A floodlight blasted at his back. He looked round frantically. The light was so bright he could hardly see where it was coming from. He blinked rapidly and made out the silhouette of a small patrol boat, with two or perhaps three figures on it.

They've got me, he thought. *It's over.* But at the

same time, there was a seed of warmth growing in his belly. It exploded through his muscles and when it reached Jimmy's brain he thought he heard his own voice shouting, issuing commands. *Move!* he told himself. *They've seen me, but if they knew who I was they'd have shot me already.*

Somehow, Jimmy found another level of strength and speed. But he was like a helpless insect caught in a web.

"Do not move!" the loudspeaker repeated. "This is a restricted area controlled by the British Government! Do not move or we will be forced to shoot."

Jimmy let each word fuel his determination to reach the top before they could stop him. Then, over the noise of the wind and the machinery of the rig, Jimmy picked up the distinctive click of a rifle. That same instant, he hooked his foot through the lattice of the metal strut and let his body fall backwards. A bullet pinged off the metal, right where Jimmy's heart had been just a second before.

Jimmy tightened his thigh muscle and swung himself to position the metal strut between him and the patrol boat. He moved fast, never pausing. The floodlight followed him. Then came two more shots. They both hit the metal in front of Jimmy's face, throwing sparks into his mask. Now there was only a metre between Jimmy and the underside of the rig platform. There was a horizontal rack of scaffolding and a hatch directly above him, with no time to worry about what might be on the other side of it.

He dragged himself on to the scaffolding. One sharp smack with his elbow sent the hatch flying open. Jimmy dived through it, landing with a roll. He found himself in a black corridor made completely of metal. Jimmy was in the corner of the rig and the tunnel ran in two directions away from him.

The place was full of frantic shouts and the hammering of boots. The air was so thick with the smell of oil it felt almost solid when Jimmy breathed. And towards him, from both directions, came hurtling two sets of dancing torchlights. There was no way of telling how many men were behind them – or how many guns.

Jimmy didn't wait to see what they were going to do. There was only one way to go – up. The roof of the corridor was low and lined with pipes. Jimmy jumped to catch one, then crunched his stomach muscles to bring himself up and catch the pipe between his knees. He smashed the metal above him – this time with both elbows at the same time.

A panel in the ceiling came free and Jimmy rolled through on to the floor above. Now there was space to run. He pelted down the corridor that ran the length of one side of the base. The soles of Jimmy's wetsuit squeaked on the metal panels under his feet. He felt the impact of every step. All around him was the noise of boots beating out the chase through metal corridors. They were closing in from every direction.

As he ran, Jimmy took in his surroundings, trying to work out how he could hide. Every few metres another camera seemed to taunt him with a blinking red light. There was nowhere he could go that he wouldn't be seen. This was going as badly as Jimmy could have imagined – he was nowhere near the central hall and he'd already been caught on camera about a dozen times. His mask might hide his face and distort his features from the heat sensors, but what good was that when his physique was obviously a child's?

Jimmy slid round a corner. There was an opening in the wall and he ducked through it. Now, instead of being in an enclosed tunnel, Jimmy found himself in a labyrinth of metal walkways, ladders and struts. The walkways had open sides with just a handrail, so he could see up and down on to the other levels, and the floor panels were grilled with tiny holes.

The place seemed to be a giant cube and Jimmy was near the bottom of it, but in every direction it looked the same. That gave him an idea. He leaned back and kicked out at the handrail. Two sharp blows loosened a railing and Jimmy yanked the metal bar free, wincing at the agony in his fingers.

He swung the bar at the camera, smashing it to pieces with one blow, then scrabbled around on the floor, carefully picking up fragments of the camera's lens. It took all his concentration to shape his fingers well enough to grip the pieces of glass, but he managed it.

"Freeze!" came a shout from behind him.

Jimmy didn't even bother to look round. He swept his leg back and across the floor, connecting with a man's ankles. He kept rotating and ducked his shoulder into the man's knees as he fell. His opponent tumbled over him, off the walkway, and crashed into the metal one floor down.

Jimmy leapt up and dashed to the next camera. He knew he only had a few seconds before another security agent arrived – and this time they'd shoot him. He stood with his back to the wall and the camera directly above his head. Then he reached up with the largest fragment of glass and jammed it sideways into the front of the camera's lens. He quickly took a smaller piece of glass and balanced it at an angle on top of the first.

It took him two attempts, but he did it – he'd reflected the camera's view so that it was looking the wrong way down the corridor. Both views were the same, so anybody watching the monitor wouldn't notice the difference. In effect, Jimmy had created a small section of the walkway where he could be invisible.

That's where he ran now. He checked to see that there was no other camera watching him, then carefully lowered himself over the edge. There he found a supporting iron girder running lengthways along the underside of the walkway. There was a sliver of a gap on top of it, underneath the floor Jimmy had been standing on a second ago. That gap was enough.

Jimmy slid into the dark space and lay flat on his back. That moment, a dozen men hurtled along the walkway directly above Jimmy's face. He saw the soles of their boots through the tiny holes in the metal.

But they couldn't see him. As far as base security was concerned, the intruder had disappeared as mysteriously as he'd arrived. For the time being, Jimmy could hide here and wait for his fingers to recover well enough for him to complete his mission. Now all he had to do was work out how to do that, and get away from Neptune's Shadow alive.

18 THE WRONG SABOTEUR

"What do you mean, missing?" Miss Bennett blasted into the phone. "How can an intruder go missing? Check the surveillance footage!" She listened to the frantic voice at the other end of the line and the grimace on her face grew deeper.

Eva tapped the stylus on the screen of her palmtop nervously. Whenever Miss Bennett received bad news, Eva bore the brunt of her temper. Within the concrete walls of NJ7, there was nowhere to escape her anger.

Miss Bennett slammed the phone down, but picked it straight back up again, dialling a single digit. "Tell the PM I'm coming to see him," she barked. "No – NOW!" The receiver got another slamming. Eva wondered how many phones Miss Bennett had broken in her time at the Secret Service.

"Come on, Eva," Miss Bennett barked, jumping up

from behind her desk. "We've got an appointment at Number 10."

By now, Eva was used to rushing through the NJ7 corridors at Miss Bennett's pace, and marched just behind her boss. One thing she didn't think she'd ever get used to, though, was the fact that her best friend's dad was now Prime Minister. Every time they went to see him at 10 Downing Street, Eva felt the stress bursting to get out of her. But she couldn't release it.

The world had changed for all of them since the days when she would go round to hang out at Georgie Coates's house. Eva was with NJ7 now and had to act like it. Putting Georgie out of her mind was the hardest thing she'd ever had to do.

Together, Miss Bennett and Eva charged through the heavy metal door that was the direct entrance to Number 10 from the NJ7 bunkers. A Downing Street aide was there to escort them into the PM's study.

"I just received a call from the MoD," Miss Bennett announced, not bothering with hellos. "An intruder has breached security at Neptune's Shadow."

Ian Coates was standing by the window, framed by the dark green, floral curtains and silhouetted against the bright light filtering through the lace.

"That's between you and the Ministry of Defence," he replied, not turning round. His voice was infused with irritation. "It's no reason to interrupt my schedule." Only now did he spin on his heels to look at them. "I don't just twiddle my thumbs waiting for you to turn up, you know."

"The intruder has disappeared," Miss Bennett replied. "A child."

"Zafi?" Coates asked.

"Who else?"

"Indeed." Ian Coates thought for a moment, his annoyed expression not changing. He looked from Miss Bennett to Eva, and Eva shuddered slightly, uncomfortable in his gaze.

"So send Mitchell," he said at last, with a shrug.

"Of course I'm going to send Mitchell," Miss Bennett snapped. "He's already on the Zafi assignment anyway. I'll send him with an SAS assault squad."

"So what do you want from me – a pat on the back?" He prowled across the room and took his tea from the desk, cradling the saucer in one hand while he raised the porcelain cup to his lips with the other.

"Put me in charge of the Ministry of Defence," Miss Bennett ordered.

Ian Coates almost choked on his tea, but quickly composed himself. "Oh I see," he said calmly. "So you called me out of a meeting with the Public Information Minister just to ask for a promotion?"

"I can't respond quickly enough if I receive intelligence second-hand. I need the MoD to be under NJ7 control."

Ian Coates raised an eyebrow. "You want power."

"I have power. What I need is efficiency."

The Prime Minister didn't react. Eva was amazed at how calm this man was. He seemed so assured and comfortable with the responsibility of running Britain. Perhaps it was the homely surroundings, but Eva could imagine him declaring war as easily as he'd announce what was for dinner.

"Have a drink with me," he said at last, his voice low and flat.

"What?" Miss Bennett gasped.

"Have a drink with me and you can have control over every military arm of this government."

This was the first time Eva had seen Miss Bennett looking out of her depth. Her steady stare had vanished and instead her eyes flitted around the room awkwardly.

"I'll get Mitchell on a helicopter," she announced, turning to leave. "Come on, Eva."

Eva smiled sheepishly at the Prime Minister and followed Miss Bennett out of the room, tapping as quickly as she could on her palmtop.

"Stop that," Miss Bennett snapped at Eva. "There's no need to type up that conversation."

The Prime Minister's aide put her head round the door into his study. "The Public Information Minister is still here, sir," she said softly. "Do you want him to wait?"

"No," Ian Coates mumbled and waved her out. He stared out of the window while he finished his tea. Miss Bennett had granted him a rare interruption in his schedule, but beneath his serene appearance, his mind was racing. He reached into his trouser pocket and pressed the button on a tiny beeper.

A few seconds later, the bookshelf at the back of the room slid into the wall. Behind it was a dark passageway. Out of the shadows marched a giant man. His jaw caught the light first and he looked so imposing he could have been a Roman emperor, if it hadn't been for the full military uniform.

"What do you think, Paduk?" the Prime Minister asked.

"I think you should know a woman's first name before you ask her out for a drink, sir." Paduk tried to hide his smile.

"Not about that," Coates sighed.

"Sorry, sir." The smile vanished. "What I meant was, *HMS Euphemus* is docked in Vlissingen. She can be there in forty-five minutes."

"What's a battle cruiser going to do now someone is already inside?" Coates asked. "No. Mitchell's the best weapon to combat this."

"Sir, with respect, the child-assassin project has shown how unreliable it can be." Paduk's voice was uncertain. He wasn't used to challenging the Prime

Minister. "To carry on using Mitchell at a time of crisis is at best risky and at worst..."

"At worst what?"

"Well..." Paduk gathered himself, then announced, "It's cruel."

"*Cruel?*" Ian Coates could hardly believe what he had heard.

"We thought they'd be machines," Paduk insisted, careful to avoid eye contact. "But I've trained with them. And I've seen them at work. In the future, I don't know – maybe they'll become assassins. But for now Mitchell's still just a child."

"Just a child?" Coates stormed. "Mitchell is our greatest asset. And Zafi is our greatest threat. Don't forget, I've seen them at work too – the other one nearly killed me."

"The other one?" Paduk nearly choked on his words. "Do you mean Jimmy?"

The Prime Minister was silent. He turned away.

"Or don't we say that name any more?" Paduk whispered.

"Stop," said Ian Coates firmly.

Paduk's face flickered and he let out a barely audible growl.

"If you have something to say about that boy," said the Prime Minister, glaring over his shoulder, "keep it to yourself."

Paduk pursed his lips. But then the words flew out of him. "We tricked him, trapped him and shot him. As if he was an animal. The second he died, we became monsters."

"STOP!" Coates yelled, stepping up to Paduk. "I'm ordering you!" The two men were almost nose to nose.

Paduk dropped his gaze. He was breathing hard. "Sorry, sir," he rasped. Then he stepped back and straightened his uniform.

For a few seconds there was silence. Neither man looked at the other. Then, at last, the Prime Minister spoke, but he couldn't hide the tremor in his voice. "The New York operation was a success. The threat was neutralised. We did it for Great Britain."

"Did Great Britain deserve it?" Paduk whispered.

The Prime Minister's glare was full of shock and venom. "Sometimes great men must do terrible things for a higher purpose," he said, as if quoting from memory. "That is what makes them great."

Paduk didn't respond, but looked down at his shoes. Ian Coates paused for a moment and shook his head, as if trying to get rid of whatever he was thinking. Then he turned back to Paduk. "But you're right in one way. We can't take any risks. And Mitchell has failed before, so... I want you to go as well."

A flicker of confusion came over Paduk's face. "Sir, my job is here."

"Your job is protecting the country," Coates insisted.

"Are you testing my loyalty?"

"Should I be?"

Paduk didn't answer, so the Prime Minister carried on. "If anything happens to Neptune's Shadow..." Coates sucked air between his teeth. "Well, that is out of the question. If Mitchell fails again, I want you there to back him up." He moved right up to Paduk, made sure the man was looking him in the eye, then whispered, "Whatever happens, the French must not sabotage Neptune's Shadow. Understand?"

Paduk took a deep breath and cracked his jaw.

"I'll call for a chopper, sir."

19 *THE WRONG INSTINCT*

Mitchell hunched forward with his coat collar turned up round his ears. He was the only figure on the line of a dozen benches at the edge of Lake Tjornin, in the centre of Reykjavik. He tossed a few crumbs on to the concrete at his feet and was soon surrounded by geese. Some of them were so fat Mitchell wondered whether they could still fly.

He glanced up every few seconds at City Hall, watching everybody that went in or out. It was an impressive modernist structure that backed on to the water. Its stone columns blended perfectly into the grey of the water. In fact, everything about Lake Tjornin was an even grey except for white explosions of goose droppings.

If Zafi had wanted to slip out of Iceland unnoticed, it would have been impossible to stop her. *So why haven't I left too?* Mitchell asked himself. Something had held him back, as if he could smell Zafi on the cool Icelandic breeze.

There had to be a reason she'd come back to Europe through Iceland, he reasoned. Why not fly straight home to France? Or if she was planning some kind of operation in Britain, why not go straight there? Mitchell had only been able to track her to Iceland because a shop assistant at JFK airport had been accused of stealing from the till. It was a stroke of luck that Zafi turned up on the security footage and an MI6 agent was in place to see it.

So she could have picked any country in the world to escape to. And she had come here. Mitchell's programming hummed inside him, warming his blood but not offering any new ideas. For the first time he felt like trading in some of his assassin skills for a little extra brain power.

His thoughts were interrupted by a dull vibration in his jacket pocket. He pulled out a silver mobile phone and flipped it open.

"I'm at City Hall," he said softly.

"And I'm at the end of my tether," Miss Bennett's voice snapped back down the phone.

"No, listen," Mitchell pleaded. "I don't think she's left the country. I think she came for, like, political reasons. You know, to kill someone. I don't know. I need you to brief me on possible French targets in Iceland."

"Leave the politics to me," Miss Bennett barked. "Your job is not to reason things out, however rational you think you're being. You're not a rational creature. You obey orders. Orders from me and orders from your... instincts."

"But this *is* an instinct," Mitchell insisted.

"Then it's the wrong instinct. Your programming must be—"

"This wasn't my—" Mitchell stopped himself. He knew he had failed again. There was no way of hiding it from Miss Bennett.

"There's a chopper coming to pick you up," she announced. "Your target's been spotted."

"Spotted?" Mitchell's heart bucked with the excitement of a hungry carnivore. "Where?"

"The middle of the North Sea."

"The North Sea?" Mitchell gasped.

"You'll be fully briefed once you're in transit."

"But it doesn't make sense," Mitchell protested. "How could she have got there so fast? I'm telling you, she's still in Reykjavik."

"To kill someone?" Miss Bennett's voice dripped with sarcasm.

"Well... Maybe... Or, I don't know... Maybe she stayed to make some kind of alliance... That's why I'm—"

"Listen to me, Mitchell Glenthorne. No French

trollop is going to make a secret alliance with the Icelandic Government. As long as we let the Icelanders fish our waters, they'll be on our side. And as for the French wanting to kill someone there..." She paused for breath. The earpiece of Mitchell's phone was growing hot with her fury. "What possible target could she have at Reykjavik City Hall? Do you know how big the Icelandic army is?"

Mitchell muttered something under his breath.

"One," Miss Bennett went on, at full force. "One man. That's it. And I happen to know that right now that man is in Barbados with our Foreign Secretary's wife. That's classified by the way, Mitchell. Nobody else needs to know. But if you think he's going to launch a one-man invasion..."

"OK, OK," Mitchell sighed. He pushed down his embarrassment and humiliation. They were human weaknesses. He stood up and hurled the rest of his bread into the water, causing a riot of goose squawks. He delved deep for his programming.

"Where do I meet the chopper?"

Jimmy had no idea how long he had been hiding, flat on his back on this iron girder. It was long enough for his hands to have recovered a little. Unfortunately, now that the feeling was returning, a throbbing agony came too. He tried to flex his fingers and raised his right arm as slowly as he could. Any movement could give away his hiding place.

Through the mesh in the metal directly above him he could see troops pounding the walkway, searching the base. He could hear them passing below him as well, on the lower level, but didn't dare turn to look.

They would have known about the smashed surveillance camera straightaway – perhaps they even watched him do it. How long did Jimmy have before they found the modification he had made to the next camera along? Before then, Jimmy needed to be back in shape and ready for action.

He tried to work out which direction he had to go to find the central hall. He closed his eyes and conjured up perfect recollections of the photographs from the spy plane. But they were aerial photos. They couldn't tell him which way to go from where he was hiding now. Instead, he tried to remember his exact route since coming on to the base. Thinking about it took his mind off the throbbing in his fingers and the spikes digging into his face inside his mask.

I'm out of time, he thought. *Forget the pain. Move now.* His eyes shot open. He still didn't have a clear idea of the way to the missiles, but he was going to have to make the best of it.

He took a deep breath, filling his nostrils with the

bitter flavour of oil. He pressed his eye up to one of the holes in the metal above him, waited to make sure that the passageway was clear, then carefully turned over on to his front. The girder was only the width of his shoulders, but it ran the length of the walkway. As long as Jimmy was on it, he would be above the scope of the surveillance cameras on the level below, and hidden from the camera on the level above by the walkway itself.

He shuffled along the beam, slowly at first, and eventually made his way to the end of the passage. The beam ran straight into the wall, with nowhere for Jimmy to go.

He had a choice – drop to the floor of the level below him or climb on to the walkway above. Either way he'd be spotted instantly on camera. On both levels there was a metal door at the end of the walkway.

Suddenly, the walkway above him started vibrating. Jimmy froze. Then the door on that level burst open and a dozen men rushed out. They were looking for him, and their boots were close enough for Jimmy to read their shoe sizes off the leather soles.

Jimmy felt something rumbling inside him, making his muscles twitch. His body had recognised an opportunity. In the instant that the last man ran overhead, Jimmy grabbed the edge of the walkway above him. He pulled himself round it, on to the level above, and rolled through the metal door as it clanged shut. The group of men had shielded him from the view of the cameras. He'd made it through unseen.

But it was the wrong door. Instead of finding himself in another corridor, with a clear way to the centre of the base, Jimmy stood up in a dingy and cramped common room. There was a table covered in newspapers and empty crisp packets, and the walls were lined with computers. On one of the screens was a half-finished game of minesweeper.

Jimmy looked around in desperation. The one thing this room didn't have was another way out. It was a dead end and any second one of those men could be coming back.

20 OFFSHORE SHUFFLE

Jimmy was about to rush back out into the passageway, but his fingers trembled on the door handle. He knew it was the wrong decision.

He turned back to the room and studied every corner for anything that could help him. His eyes fell on a mobile phone lying next to an open magazine. Jimmy didn't need his programming to know he could use it for something – but he struggled to work out exactly what. Then he noticed a wire that entered the room above the door, ran down the corner and connected to what looked like an ordinary fuse box fixed to the wall. The lock was rusting and Jimmy easily broke it open.

Inside was a complex circuit board with the single cable entering at the top. At the other end was a black cube with a short aerial and a flashing red light. There was only one thing that cable could have been connected to outside in the passageway – the surveillance cameras.

Jimmy smiled so hard the prongs in his mask almost twisted out of shape. He didn't care. At last one piece of luck had gone his way. He'd stumbled across the transformer that beamed the signal from the cameras back to the control centre, where the security team would be watching their screens.

Jimmy grabbed the mobile phone and quickly found the video function. Then he pulled the door open just a sliver and held the phone up to the crack. He kept it there for as long as he dared, filming the empty passageway outside. A few seconds was enough. He closed the door again and snapped the plastic casing off the back of the phone.

Now he turned to the box on the wall and searched inside himself for help. He knew to rely on his instincts to guide him through the electrical system. For his programming, it was a simple matter to rewire the circuit board to incorporate the new video clip. For his hands it wasn't so easy. It was a delicate process and his fingers shook as he worked.

He wiped the sweat from the back of his neck. He was amazed at what he seemed to be capable of, without his conscious mind having the slightest understanding of what his hands were doing. At school, physics had been one of his weakest subjects. Now he was relying on it to save his life. At last he finished piecing together a new circuit. It cut off the true input from the cameras and replaced it with the looped images of the same empty passageway.

He wedged the phone next to the black cube and gingerly closed the lid of the circuit box. It wasn't perfect – as soon as anybody examined it closely, Jimmy's alteration would be discovered. But Jimmy hoped it was good enough for now. All he needed was enough time to find the missiles.

He tore out into the open, pounding along the walkways. He stretched every muscle in his legs, forcing his stride longer and longer, straining to reach the missiles before security shot him down. He could already picture himself disarming Britain's weapons. He imagined Miss Bennett's face when she found out what had happened. He saw Ian Coates, his plans for war with France set back or even finished.

But then Jimmy's memory flashed to the image of Bligh, just before he fell from the plane – the shard of glass sticking out of his cheek, the calm resignation in his eyes. Jimmy's gut twisted with terror all over again. He was here as much for that dead agent as for the populations of Britain and France – or even his own family and friends.

Jimmy charged through a door and found himself in the vast central hall of the base. Despite it being open to the elements, the air was noticeably warmer. That was because of the machinery. Six massive metal cylinders gave off a loud hum. Each one was about fifteen metres across and they towered all the way up to the top of the hall, which Jimmy thought must have been more than a hundred metres up.

Jimmy recognised the cylinders from the aerial photographs. On those images, they'd shown up as six grey blobs in the centre of the base. Were these the missiles? Jimmy ran up to one of the tanks and circled it, looking for some kind of launch mechanism in its base.

Then he peered up the walls of the tank. Scaffolding and open-sided walkways lined the whole hall, and at every level there was some kind of control unit where a walkway met a tank. A light drizzle speckled Jimmy's visor as he tried to make out what it said on the control panels.

The tanks didn't look as Jimmy had expected, but perhaps that shouldn't have been a surprise. After all, if the base was a converted oil rig, and still disguised as one, then the missiles themselves would probably be hidden in machinery that used to be for oil. These tanks were easily big enough to conceal the entire missile mechanism inside them and some of them may even still contain oil. In fact, the smell of oil was now so strong that it was an effort to breathe.

Then a shudder ripped through Jimmy's body. He heard a drone beneath the rumble of the machinery. He looked up, dreading what he suspected he would see.

There it was – a powerful floodlight from a huge

military helicopter. The beam burned into the floor of the hall. Then Jimmy saw the silhouette of six black coils twisting out of the choppers. The ropes swished through the air until they were totally extended, hanging about five metres from the floor. Then came the outlines of a dozen big men, two sliding down each rope at amazing speed. Their backs curved round, making them look like giant beetles – beetles with assault rifles.

Jimmy gulped. Now it was obvious why base security had cleared out of the central hall. They were making way for the SAS.

Jimmy was terrified. Every muscle froze. He wanted to move, but was transfixed by the soldiers whizzing down towards him. A normal boy would have been finished right then. But a normal boy would never have made it there in the first place and Jimmy wasn't about to give up.

He felt a torrent of power surge through his legs. Suddenly, he was moving again, and with the precision of a deadly snake. He darted to the side of the hall and leapt up the scaffolding. In two seconds he was several metres off the ground and still climbing. Then he felt the heat of torch beams on the back of his neck. He knew what would come next – the rip of SAS machine guns.

Without even looking round, Jimmy launched himself off the scaffolding with such force that it felt like his stomach had been left behind. He stretched his arms out over his head and grabbed one of the SAS ropes.

Jimmy swung full circle round the rope. There was one SAS man above him, one below him. That meant neither could shoot at Jimmy for fear of hitting the other man. The cord slid through Jimmy's hands. He willed his body to swamp the pain. He spiralled down in complete control, shoved his foot into the face of the soldier beneath him and used it as a trampoline to bounce back up.

The SAS man above him jumped off the rope just before Jimmy could reach him. The other soldiers did the same and clambered up the scaffolding all round the hall. They were vying for the perfect shot.

Jimmy was surrounded. He glanced up. Through the glare of the floodlight, he just made out another marksman still in the helicopter. Jimmy was a sitting duck.

The sights of the guns peppered his body. His nerves were anticipating where the first bullet would hit. What would it feel like? Jimmy had thought he'd been shot a couple of times, but it had never actually happened. What were his chances of avoiding it now? Even worse, Jimmy then realised why the soldier in the helicopter hadn't shot him already – he was busy untying the rope. After a crash-landing on the floor, Jimmy would be an even easier target.

He swung his legs violently, swaying further and further, turning the rope into a giant pendulum. Jimmy swung through the air. Then, just as he felt the rope come free from its fastening in the chopper, he swirled it round above his head and hurled one end towards the top of the nearest storage tank.

The instant before Jimmy hit the ground, the end of the rope wrapped itself round one of the struts of scaffolding, right at the top of the hall. It went taut and Jimmy swung on the end, his knees sweeping the floor. He pumped his legs, moving in massive leaps round the walls, using the impetus of his fall to defy gravity.

That's when the SAS opened fire.

21 NEPTUNE'S VOLCANO

Assault rifles roared, blasting through the sounds of the machinery. Bullets smacked against the scaffolding, always just where Jimmy had been a split-second before. He had to keep running. But there was one problem.

Every bullet that hit the metal scaffolding sent up a bright orange spark – and the air was thick with oil fumes. As suddenly as they'd started, the soldiers stopped shooting. A big enough spark could cause even worse sabotage than Jimmy would have been able to manage on his own. Their commanding officer must have realised – but it was too late.

Jimmy kept running round the walls, circling the entire hall, swinging on the rope. He glanced down, just in time to see a river of golden flames erupting across the lower levels of scaffolding.

As one, the SAS soldiers started climbing again. There was no way down now. The fire moved so fast

Jimmy thought it was a bolt of lightning. In no time, the floor of the hall was an inferno. The heat was so intense it burned the inside of his mouth as he breathed. Without his mask, Jimmy knew his face would have blistered. The light was so bright below him that at first he couldn't look. Instead, he saw the flashing orange illuminating the black SAS figures as they clambered higher and higher for safety. The team of Britain's fighting elite were reboarding their chopper.

When he finally did look down, Jimmy realised why their priority had changed from killing him to surviving. The flames were licking the outsides of the storage tanks. If Jimmy was wrong and these giant units didn't contain missiles, but were actually vast lakes of oil… He didn't want to imagine the destruction.

Jimmy pulled himself into the scaffolding. He pelted along the walkways, climbing to the next level at every opportunity. He knew his only chance was to somehow escape on the helicopter. Getting away on a chopper full of his enemy wouldn't be easy, but it had to be better than staying on the inside of an erupting volcano.

He wiped his visor. The edges were blackened from the flames and the base's sprinkler system was blasting him with water. Even with the help of the rain, it didn't seem to be controlling the flames, but it was certainly making it hard for Jimmy to see where he was going. There were only two levels above him now. He kept running.

A siren blasted through the noise of the fire, but Jimmy blanked it out to concentrate on the steady patter of his strides. His breathing stung his throat. Black smoke was everywhere and it was growing thicker by the second.

Even while he choked for air, Jimmy realised that he might have saved thousands of lives. He still didn't know whether the missiles were inside these tanks, but wherever they were hidden, surely the base would at least be too damaged to fire them. More likely, it would be destroyed completely. All Jimmy had to do now was find a way to safety.

He reached the top level of the central hall just in time to see the last of the SAS soldiers boarding the chopper. Jimmy didn't know what to do. There was no way to catch the helicopter's runner without the SAS seeing him and shooting him down.

His hesitation was already too long. He'd been spotted.

The helicopter lifted slowly from its hover position, almost camouflaged against the clouds. But before it could zip away, a small figure leapt out of the cabin. It landed with a roll right on top of the largest of the storage tanks. It was covered head to toe in black combat gear and the face was masked, but from the body shape,

Jimmy knew exactly who it had to be – Mitchell.

"Come on!" Mitchell shouted, though his words were barely audible over the noise. The smoke was so thick now that it even shut out the view of the helicopter. But as the smog blustered in the wind of the chopper's rotor, it cleared for long enough for Jimmy to see that Mitchell was looking straight at him.

Jimmy couldn't be shot at – the smoke was too thick to see him and there was too much risk of blowing up the whole base. So Mitchell had come down to make sure he didn't leave his job unfinished this time. He raised both hands and beckoned Jimmy on. For a second, Jimmy's whole body trembled. It wasn't the fear. It was the knowledge that Mitchell would recognise him. His cover might already have been blown when the SAS saw him, but now it was definite. NJ7 would know he was still alive.

Jimmy dug deep for his last reserves of strength and tried to push away his feelings. He ran round the edge of the walkway away from Mitchell, gathering pace. From this top level, he could look down to his right into the fire at the centre of the hall, but to his left was a view over the sea.

For a second at a time, clearings in the smog opened up. Jimmy caught a glimpse of a parade of small boats hurrying away with everybody who had been evacuated off the base. *We're the only ones left*, he thought. *Nobody to save but myself.*

Jimmy turned to climb out over the walkway railing and make his way down to the water. But something locked on to his ankles.

It was Mitchell's hand.

Every one of the SAS troops clung to the walls of the cabin inside the helicopter. They'd all pulled their helmets over their eyes and strapped themselves tightly to their seats. With every shake of the aircraft, they grimaced and groaned.

They were all experienced servicemen who'd flown in war zones and assault situations many times before. But tonight, the EC7025 Cougar was hovering above a cauldron. Currents of hot air surged up from under them, tipping the chopper from side to side. Meanwhile, isolated pockets of cold hit them out of nowhere, dragging them down. Any second the pilot could lose control, either plunging them down into the flames or, just as bad, letting the wind flip them over and hurl them violently out to sea. None of the SAS team had ever experienced a flight that was so dangerous, for so long.

Only one soldier seemed unaware of the extreme turbulence. He was by far the biggest man there. The corners of his jaw jutted out sharply, making his balaclava look like a black box with two diamonds peeking out of the eye holes. Paduk wasn't even strapped in. He was leaning out of the cabin, peering down into the cloud, hardly blinking. With every opening, he searched for a glimpse of the two child assassins fighting below.

He gasped at the strength and agility of the two figures – and how similar they were. With both of them head-to-toe in black, it was even harder to be sure which was which. Paduk was fascinated by the sight of near mirror images locked in combat. Even though one of them was bigger, they both had the same precision in the movement of every muscle, the same resilience when they were struck, and the same techniques to try and deceive their opponent.

It was like watching a computer game, where two characters might look slightly different, but are governed by the same rules, the same constraints. *Of course*, Paduk thought. *The same programming.*

Mitchell hurled Jimmy round his head and let go. Jimmy flew through the blackness, huge flames flaring beneath him. He landed in an awkward roll across the roof of one of the storage tanks. Mitchell followed, slamming down barely two metres away.

Jimmy jumped to his feet. For a split-second they

both froze, sizing up their opponent. They may as well have been the only two people in the world now, isolated in a metal circle about fifteen metres across.

Then Mitchell charged. Jimmy set his muscles, ready for anything. His attacker loomed out of the black smoke like a rhino from the jungle.

Jimmy twisted his hips and dipped his shoulders back. His right leg snapped up at Mitchell's head. Mitchell dropped to the floor, where the metal was greasy with rain. He slid underneath Jimmy's counterattack and jammed his elbow into the back of Jimmy's ankle. Jimmy pitched backwards, but caught his balance in time to turn his fall into an elegant back flip. He landed squarely on both feet. Mitchell had disappeared into the smoke.

Every fibre in Jimmy's body was on alert. He swivelled, trying to spot his enemy. Then suddenly, Mitchell burst out of the darkness. Jimmy dug his heels into a rivet in the metal and turned his shoulder to absorb the blow. Mitchell barrelled into him. It was like being hit by a cannon ball. Jimmy's entire skeleton rattled. He was thrown over Mitchell's back and crashed to the floor.

For a second he couldn't move. Even his lungs refused to pull in a breath. The throbbing in his bones told him that Mitchell's assassin abilities had developed even in the short time since they'd last fought.

At last Jimmy pushed himself up, but he wasn't steady. The metal beneath him was moving. The lid of this huge tank was sliding open – and quickly. Jimmy fell to his knees. Then a massive flame blazed up past him, blowing a clearing in the smoke. Through the orange flash, Jimmy saw Mitchell running from one of the control panels. He'd opened the tank.

A gulf was rapidly widening between Jimmy and Mitchell. Jimmy looked down into the tanker. Despite the danger, a small part of him was still fascinated to look inside. Even before he could see, it was obvious what the tank contained. The fumes smacked Jimmy in the face.

That's when he knew he had been wrong.

No missiles were concealed inside this tank. Sure enough, several metres below him was a black disc, shining back with a perfect reflection – the surface of thousands of litres of oil. It was beautiful. And it was lethal.

Then, in the reflection, Jimmy saw Mitchell being lifted away into the sky, holding the runner of the helicopter with one hand. Jimmy looked up. He was revolted by the other boy's smug, exaggerated wave. He saw that Mitchell was shouting something. With all the other noise, it wasn't hard for Jimmy to ignore Mitchell's taunting. What could he possibly be saying that Jimmy would want to hear?

But Mitchell was enjoying it too much and persisted in screaming at the top of his lungs. Something about it made Jimmy's skin prickle. He listened closer. He tried to study Mitchell's lips, but in seconds he was too far away and then the smoke cut off Jimmy's view.

The echo of Mitchell's laugh remained, along with his words. Jimmy could hardly believe it, but now he realised what Mitchell had been shouting:

"Goodbye, Zafi!"

Jimmy felt a lurch of elation. His hands jumped to his mask. In the fight he'd completely forgotten that he was so well covered.

He gritted his teeth, with a new determination to survive. Mitchell hadn't been able to finish him off – again. If Jimmy could get out of here, he would still have the protection that NJ7 thought he had been killed in New York.

Unfortunately, Jimmy had nowhere to go. The floor was vanishing under his feet, retracting into the side of the storage tank. He was right at the edge now, looking out over the oil inside, and moving further and further from the walkway. He couldn't jump down the other way – even without the massive fire, it was too great a fall.

Jimmy stood there, helpless. Then he gathered his courage and set himself to make the leap across the oil to the walkway. He only had room for a run-up of a single step.

It'll have to do, he thought. He clenched his knees, swung his arms to gain momentum and sprang into the air.

Jimmy stretched every muscle, urging his body to fly just a little further. *It's not so far*, he told himself. *I can make it*. He reached up, straining to catch the opposite edge of the tank.

But the jump was further than it looked. He splashed into the black, glutinous pool. It was heavy on his limbs and surprisingly warm. With every movement, a curtain of black liquid stuck to him. *It's OK*, Jimmy told himself. *I can swim through it*. If he could make if to the edge of the tank, he might be able to climb out.

But Jimmy knew that the tank was being heated by the fire. Crude oil wouldn't have been so dangerous, but this oil had been refined on site, then piped to these tanks for storage. If it grew hot enough, it would reach flashpoint. As soon as that happened, Jimmy may as well be swimming inside the biggest petrol bomb ever built.

22 BLACK DEATH

Paduk remembered his training runs with Mitchell. He'd been startled by how the boy could seem totally vulnerable one minute, then like a lethal machine the next. Watching him now, Paduk saw how much the machine had taken control. It disgusted him. He spat a fat globule of phlegm out of the helicopter.

Monsters, he thought. *We were monsters to create them and monsters to kill one of them.* His memory toyed with him. Now, instead of seeing Mitchell on those training runs, he saw Jimmy. He even started to imagine that it was Jimmy down there fighting Mitchell, not Zafi. The similarities in style were so strong that it may as well have been.

Paduk threw off his torment with a low grunt. He had to stay focused. His top priority had been the protection of Neptune's Shadow. He'd failed. He knew that. But the mission wasn't over. The disaster could become even worse if Mitchell got himself killed. On the other hand, there could be at least one positive outcome if they eliminated the French assassin. Paduk only wished Mitchell hadn't broken ranks to try and take Zafi on alone. Perhaps the genetic assassins weren't designed to be part of an assault team.

"Take us lower!" Paduk shouted into his headset. "We're going back down."

"Forget it!" the pilot yelled back. "We can't save the place now. Look at it!"

"I know," Paduk replied. "Neptune's Shadow is finished. But we have to help Mitchell."

"Are you nuts?" The pilot glanced over his shoulder, venom in his eyes. All the time he was grappling with the controls of the Cougar, desperate to keep the flight as steady as possible. It was a losing battle. "If one more soldier leaves that cabin, there won't be time to get you all back up again. That boy was crazy to jump down there. We shouldn't even be waiting for him. More men going after him isn't just suicide – it's murdering anybody that has to wait up here for them to come back. Unless that boy gets out of there right now, we'll all be cooked alive."

"So we'd better go down there to pick him up, don't you think?"

The pilot didn't respond, but after a second he plunged the Cougar into a dive. Paduk turned to the scene below them. He saw Mitchell hitting the control panel of the storage tank and watched the roof sliding away, like the eye of a Cyclops opening after a long sleep.

"Go! Go!" Paduk bellowed. "Lower!"

Mitchell was running towards them, ready to jump.

"This is as low as we can go!" the pilot screamed back. An orange flame flared up at them.

"I'll tell you when we're as low as we can go," Paduk insisted, sweat pouring off him. He waved Mitchell forwards. Then, at last, Mitchell leapt up, snatching the runner of the Cougar with his fingertips. Paduk sighed with relief. But then he glanced up, looking through the smoke to the open tank of oil just as the figure of the other assassin plunged into the black pool. *Is that the end?* Paduk asked himself. *Has he done it?*

The helicopter rose into the sky, picking up speed. But Paduk was still transfixed by what he saw in the tank of oil. Was that the assassin's head breaking the surface? Mitchell clawed his way into the cabin and slumped down on the floor. He pulled off his balaclava, revealing a massive grin.

Paduk couldn't return the smile. "Go!" he ordered the pilot. "Don't wait for me. Get this chopper out of here."

The pilot turned round. His face was twisted in shock. "You're going back?!"

"To finish the job." Paduk scowled at Mitchell, whose smile vanished.

"But the rig's going to blow!" the pilot yelled. "How will you get off it?"

Paduk cracked his jaw. "I'll find a way."

With that, he threw himself into the black smoke. *If Mitchell fails, I fail*, he thought. *If I fail, my country is in danger.*

Nobody on the helicopter saw where he landed. Immediately, the pilot peeled off to the side, using a column of updraught to lift them over the clouds and back towards land.

Jimmy poured strength into his arms and legs, but just as he was getting used to the stronger pull needed to swim through oil, giant fins rumbled into action at the bottom of the tank, rotating faster and faster. How had Mitchell activated the stirring mechanism? Moments before, the surface of the oil had been peaceful and flat. Now it was being whisked into a whirlpool.

Jimmy pleaded with his muscles to move faster and to pull harder. He was stranded in the middle of the tank. It took every last drop of effort just to stay in one place. But beneath him, the hydraulic system was speeding up. Jimmy couldn't keep his head above the surface any more.

The black liquid swallowed him up as if it was alive.

Jimmy could see nothing. His body was spun in every direction until he didn't know which way was up any more. His breath quickly ran out. He braced himself and searched for his programming to take over. He opened his mouth and let the oil gush in. Immediately, his body convulsed with the power of the chemicals poisoning his body. Jimmy waited a split-second, expecting his lungs to start drawing energy from the liquid around him. All that happened was that his chest started heaving, exactly as if he was running out of air.

He grabbed his mask with both hands and ripped it off his face, thinking that perhaps it was somehow blocking his airways and preventing him from breathing underwater. But he wasn't underwater. He was under oil.

Jimmy was dragged down, metre by metre, faster and faster. Only now did he realise how stupid he had been. Oil and water were as different from each other as water was to air. If you can breathe in one, it doesn't mean you can breathe in the other. Jimmy shut his mouth, but too late. He was drowning.

Gradually, his thoughts became more detached. His brain was suffocating. Without oxygen, it resorted to visions of his past, mixed with strange delusions. Jimmy suddenly saw himself at the school swimming pool on a sweltering hot day. He felt the intense fear that had always stopped him going in the water. The colours in his mind were vivid and glowing brighter by the second, as if the heat of the day was melting everything.

No, Jimmy screamed at himself. *It's not a hot day. It's a fire. You're drowning in a tank of hot oil.* The vision threatened to take over again so Jimmy forced himself to focus on the blackness. That was real. Anything else was leading him to death.

Jimmy could feel his ribs squeezing against his lungs. It felt like the bones would crack in his body's desperate plea for something to breathe. Jimmy revelled in the pain. It meant he was still conscious – but he knew he wouldn't be for long.

Suddenly, Jimmy was thrown against the side of the tank. The metal on his back jogged his brain into action. He was still clutching his mask. In the blackness he felt for the prongs inside it. All the power was seeping from his muscles, but he pushed all his effort into his forearms and snapped off one of the spikes. His eyes were closing. His thoughts were blurring again. He had no time left. His body was shutting down – once and for all.

Hardly aware of what he was doing, he snapped his arm straight, jabbing the metal spike into the side of the tank. That was it – his last drop of strength gone. He slumped against the side of the tank, every muscle limp.

Somewhere in Jimmy's subconscious he was aware of the oil rushing towards him, but he could never have known that it was forcing its way through the hole he'd pierced in the side of the tank. The fire ignited the oil as it rushed out. The temperature jumped by several degrees, softening the metal and weakening the integrity of the tank.

Oil and flames gushed out. On the inside of the tank wall, Jimmy was still.

At last the level of the oil was low enough for his head to be sticking out above it. But it was too late. Jimmy's eyes were closed. He wasn't breathing. His heart had stopped. All around the tank raged a torrent of fire. Any minute, the flames would rip open the tiny hole and crash through the tank wall. Jimmy would be consumed and there was nothing he could do about it.

23 OUT OF THE FRYING PAN...

Jimmy's head rolled back. His body floated in the little oil that remained in the tank and was pushed to the other side by the swirling fins. He was completely still. No breath. No pulse. No life. A ribbon of fire whipped round the outside of the tank – then it tore through the hole in the metal. The tank wall had been breached. The remaining oil inside it ignited. In an instant, the fire blazed across the surface towards Jimmy. Any evidence that a boy called Jimmy Coates had ever existed was about to be wiped out.

But inside his ribcage, something very strange was happening. The cluster of muscles that gripped his heart had gone too many seconds without a beat. They tightened, releasing tiny amounts of lactic acid. The acid caused a chemical reaction called anaerobic glycolysis. The result was thousands of sub-microscopic hydrogen ions, which exploded right next to Jimmy's heart, like somebody turning on an electric current. In a hospital, a doctor would have pressed large metal plates against Jimmy's chest and shot electricity through him, in a last attempt to kick his heart into action. But Jimmy had a far more efficient emergency system. His heart muscles acted like a built-in defibrillator.

The whole process took less than a tenth of a second. Jimmy's chest jolted from the force of the pulse within him. One blast was enough. His mouth gaped wide and pulled in a huge gasp of air. His muscles jerked automatically. It was too fast for him to know what was happening – and had to be. His eyes shot open and he saw the fire tearing towards him.

What's this? he thought frantically. *Where am I?* His heart was pumping at hundreds of beats a minute, as if a machine gun was trying to break out of his ribcage. He felt a fierce, animal panic inside, but alongside it was the cool, mechanical calm of his physical make-up. When it had most mattered, Jimmy's body had worked just as it had been designed to.

He stretched up and grabbed a rivet in the tank wall, his arms pulling the rest of him out of the oil. His fingers dug into the rivets in the metal. He was dripping with oil and black sweat that greased his grip. He couldn't move fast enough. Furious heat blasted his back.

Jimmy pushed up and clung on to the edge of the walkway. He hung directly above the tank, his fingers locked in place. Then a flame jumped up at him. The hydraulic swivel system was still spinning. With every turn it threw flaming oil at Jimmy.

He swayed out of the way and heaved to pull himself to safety, but then, looking up, he saw a man's boot. Standing on the walkway, above the chaos, was a huge shadow with shoulders so broad and a jaw so chiselled it could have been Stonehenge come to life.

Paduk.

As he stared, Jimmy remembered the stirring mechanism of the storage tank coming on after Mitchell had flown away on the SAS helicopter. Now Jimmy understood: it was Paduk who had activated the hydraulic system.

Jimmy hoisted himself up until he could rest his elbows over the edge of the walkway floor. One more push and Jimmy would be on the walkway. But it wasn't going to be that simple.

Paduk stared down at him. Jimmy saw the flash of surprise in his eyes, illuminated by the inferno below. In the heat, the man had discarded his balaclava and now his face looked like a gargoyle from hell. But he was no stone statue.

The huge soldier reached to his side and pulled out a revolver. "Tough little girl, aren't you?" he yelled, taking aim. "Mitchell should learn to stick around and finish the job."

Jimmy could do nothing but stare at Paduk's trigger finger, hoping for another miracle. His energy was used up. His heart was still pummelling the inside of his chest. It took all his strength just to keep from disappearing into the blaze. *Come on, don't give up. You can't have gone through all of this for nothing.* But however much Jimmy tried, he just couldn't come up with anything to save himself.

He shook his head and sighed. All that was left was to wait for the bullet. Finally, he dropped his face to his sleeve to wipe away the slick of oil that completely covered his face and dripped from his hair.

"You!" Paduk gasped.

Jimmy jolted to attention. Why was Paduk hesitating? He may have been surprised to see Jimmy instead of Zafi, but that was no reason not to shoot.

"How did you survive?" Paduk's face was rigid with shock and now his finger was trembling.

Jimmy couldn't work out what the man was thinking. Was he having second thoughts about shooting?

"Why did you have to come back?" Paduk screamed. "*Why?*"

"Why do you have to shoot me?" Jimmy answered, just loud enough to be heard over the roar of the flames. He wanted to sound calm, but inside his nerves were fizzing. The gun was still pointing straight at Jimmy's head. If he tried to climb up and escape, he'd be shot. If he stayed where he was and waited for Paduk to make up his mind, he might be able to dodge the first bullet, but the second would find its target. And the third, and the fourth...

Jimmy's only chance was to attack Paduk's doubt.

"Do you remember training me?" Jimmy called out. There was no response. "You once told me that Britain needs people like us to protect her. Do you remember that?" Still Paduk stood there, arm outstretched, gun gripped tight. "That's what we do, you said – you and me. We protect our country. I came here to protect my country. The country where my family and my friends are. Is this protecting your country, Paduk? Is shooting me really for the good of the country? It's for the good of NJ7, but is it for the good of Great Britain?"

Paduk opened his mouth to speak, but stopped himself. Jimmy could see the anguish on the man's face.

"If stupid Neo-democracy is that important to you," Jimmy went on. "If you think a system that lies to its own people..." Jimmy stopped himself. He was shaking. He knew he was afraid, but this was something more. There was a passion in his voice that he hadn't expected. "A system that created me!" he yelled, tears coming to his eyes. "Nothing but one massive lie. If you think all that is worth killing for... then shoot me now. You'd only be doing your duty."

Jimmy squeezed his eyes tight shut and took a deep breath.

BANG!

Jimmy flinched. But he wasn't hit. He opened his eyes. Paduk was still standing above him, but his arm was no longer pointing at Jimmy. Instead, he'd aimed past Jimmy's shoulder, at the base of the tank below. Jimmy craned his neck. The oil was draining out, lowering the level of the fire beneath him.

Jimmy almost lost his grip on the metal, but then he felt Paduk grabbing him under the arm. The huge man raised Jimmy up and threw him down on the walkway. Through bleary eyes, Jimmy saw the hazy outline of Paduk's face. Then the man's voice floated into Jimmy's mind. He only picked up fragments of it over the noise.

"Get out of here... the tanks... Go!"

In the blackness of Jimmy's brain, the core of his human self was fighting its way through. His programming throbbed with the urge to survive, but it also dulled all his human questions. At last he pushed himself up, using the handrail round the walkway to support himself. He stared into Paduk's face.

"Get out of here!" the soldier ordered, pointing over Jimmy's shoulder, out to sea. "And never come anywhere near Britain again."

Jimmy's confusion throttled the breath in his throat. By the time he could speak, Paduk had turned and was running away from him.

"What about you?" Jimmy cried out at last.

Paduk's answer resounded off the metal of the walkway. "I'm never going back!"

"Paduk!" Jimmy shouted. But the man was gone, lost in the blackness. "Hey!" Jimmy's voice was swallowed by the noise of the inferno. He looked around frantically, then searched what he could see of the sky, but he knew the helicopter couldn't have come back to pick Paduk up. The smoke was too thick and the flames were too high.

Jimmy was jolted out of his thoughts by a gulp of smoke. He coughed violently. He was standing on the very top level of the hall, but in minutes even that would be swallowed up by the fire. He turned to the edge of the walkway that overlooked the sea. From here it was a 183-metre drop to the ocean surface. It was Jimmy's only escape route, but he hesitated. Surely he'd never survive a dive like that.

The heat on his back was incredible, urging him to jump. It felt like someone was blasting his flesh with a massive blow-torch. He looked round one last time and had to squint in the glare of the inferno. A forty-storey dive into water was better than a forty-storey dive into fire.

His knees were shaking. Was that fear or because the structure he was standing on had become so unstable? He felt like the whole of Neptune's Shadow was quaking with rage. Jimmy searched for the very root of his programming, trying to kick it into the highest gear possible. He climbed up on to the handrail, then, with a final deep breath, he jumped.

The air was immediately colder. Wind rushed into Jimmy's face, tearing at his muscles. He twisted as he fell, thinking only of how he should land. With a desperate hope, he pleaded for his programming to give him wings so he could soar away over the water, never having to crash and face the pain.

His ankles locked together automatically. His arms crossed over his chest. The blood rushed to his head. For a second he thought he was going to black out, or his ears would explode, or both. He glanced down, but immediately felt sick when he saw how far he still had to fall. Waiting to smack into the water felt like long, slow torture. He tried to keep control, but heard his own voice screaming.

Then, for a fleeting second, something caught his eye. Standing on the top walkway, perfectly still, was a dark figure. Jimmy was spinning so fast away from it he couldn't make it out exactly. It was the outline of a huge man, his hands on his hips, with a burning orange glow rising behind him. It had to be Paduk.

Why didn't he jump? Why was he just standing there? Jimmy stretched his head back to see, but he was falling too fast and too hard.

Any second Jimmy would hit the water – and it would feel like concrete. Suddenly, he was blinded by a white flash. It was all around him, as if lighting up the whole world. It flared for half a second in silence – just long enough for Jimmy to know that the remaining five storage tanks had finally reached flashpoint.

BOOM!

Jimmy felt like he'd been blasted inside out. His brain rattled inside his skull. The force of the explosion hit him like a stampeding herd. It threw him up and sideways. He hurtled through the sky, no idea which direction was up and which was down. But he knew that his plummet into the sea had been interrupted. The explosion had saved him from a fall that would surely have smashed him into pieces.

His limbs flapped around him, completely out of his control. He couldn't see anything, but felt flaming debris stabbing into him.

No, I'm covered in...

It was too late. The oil that coated his wetsuit ignited. Jimmy yelled in pain. For a second he was a flaming rag doll, rolling and twisting in the air. Then, at last, he plunged into the sea.

24 NEWS FROM AUNTIE

Felix wove through the crowd, expertly balancing his lunch tray with one hand while fending off other people's elbows with the other. When he found a space at a table, he slumped down and dug in. He didn't care where he was sitting or who he was with. He managed to completely ignore everyone around him, even when they tried speaking to him.

He didn't want to talk or get to know anybody. Out of the corner of his eye he could always see that man – a tall man in a plain black suit, with a short bushy moustache that made his face look permanently grumpy.

The agents worked in shifts, but they all blended into one for Felix – one ugly, miserable, middle-aged man. Felix knew how annoyed they must be to have joined the Secret Service and then get assigned such a stupid mission. Maybe they went round invading small countries in their spare time, he thought.

Suddenly, another lunch tray slammed on to the table right opposite him.

"At least when we were on the run the food was better," Georgie announced. Her tray only had an apple on it. She immediately started crunching. Felix shrugged and examined the brown slop in front of him, with the tired corners of pasta and vegetables trying to escape from underneath. He quite liked it.

"Eugh," Georgie went on. "How can you eat that stuff?"

Felix grinned, letting a dollop of the bolognese drop from his lips back to the plate. Georgie grimaced and looked away. Felix gave a satisfied chuckle.

"Look," Georgie said quickly, "we don't have time for this. I just came to tell you…" She pulled up her bag from the floor – a black shoulder bag covered in badges. She opened a small pocket on the front, glancing up quickly at the NJ7 agent, waiting for his view to be blocked. At just the right moment she showed Felix the corner of her mobile phone.

"Hey, did you…?" Felix cut himself off, trying to contain his excitement.

"Yeah," said Georgie, hurriedly hiding it away in her bag again and getting on with her apple. "I swapped SIM cards. You'll have to memorise my new number and everything, but at least this one won't be bugged.

And hopefully they won't notice because I'm still using the same handset."

"What if they notice they're listening to a different person's conversation?"

Georgie shrugged. "The girl I swapped with hardly talks on her phone. She only texts. They'll never realise it's not me."

Felix nodded, impressed by Georgie's switch. Now they'd be able to talk to each other without NJ7 listening in. More importantly, they'd also be able to talk to Eva.

"So did you text her?" Felix asked. "You know, *Auntie*?"

Georgie smiled. Her deep brown eyes glinted in the bright light of the hall. "Yeah," she whispered. "I think it's going to work – me and her communicating like this."

"As long as she isn't, you know..."

"Don't even say that." Georgie's face was suddenly stern.

"I didn't." Felix squirmed in his seat. "But, you know, if she's caught..."

"Shut up! I told you not to say that!"

Felix shrugged. "So what's Auntie serving for tea?" he asked.

"What?"

"You know – Auntie...?"

"Yeah, but – tea?" Georgie stared at Felix like he

was a lunatic. He was used to getting that look.

"I mean, what's she got for us," he explained. "You know, what intro?"

"Do you mean intell?" Georgie raised one eyebrow.

"OK, whatever. Intell's good too. I suppose."

Georgie shook her head in exasperation. "Whatever," she sighed. "Now listen carefully..."

"You vill say zees only vunce..."

"What are you talking about?!" Georgie threw her hands up. "You're so annoying sometimes. Will you let me just tell you what she said? This is the only place where there's enough noise for nobody to overhear us and you're wasting time with stupid voices."

Felix opened his eyes wide and put a hand over his mouth. Unfortunately, he was still holding his fork and a bit of bolognese lodged in his hair. Georgie ignored it and carried on.

"I asked Auntie about the guys following us. She says they're not even proper agents. Miss Bennett doesn't think it's worth sending real ones after you and me, so these guys are just, like, regular security guards or something." She nodded in the direction of the man with the moustache who was leaning against the wall, daydreaming. "But apparently Miss Bennett thinks even that is a waste of money so the level of alert will be downgraded any day. Then we'll only be watched by one of the teachers here."

Felix clenched a fist in triumph.

"Yeah, I know," Georgie agreed. "And Auntie's going to find out which teacher it is."

"They're so stupid," Felix said in a low voice. "They should be watching us the whole time."

"Why?" Georgie asked. "What are we going to do? Take over the country without them noticing?"

Felix considered it for a moment.

"Well, we can't," Georgie added. "If we do anything except turn up for school and go home again, they'll notice. And Auntie says they'll still be monitoring all our communication, in case..." She dropped her voice and masked her hand with her mouth. "In case Jimmy isn't really dead and tries to get in touch."

"Except now they'll be monitoring the wrong phone."

Georgie beamed with pride, but the smile quickly faded.

"The only person they're watching closely twenty-four hours a day is Mum," she continued. "They know she's looking for Chris, and they know that she probably knows all the places he'd hide." She hesitated, then added, "I reckon it's true."

"What?"

"Mum probably knows all the places where Chris would hide, and where he'd look after Saffron, but she can't go there or get in touch because she'd lead Miss Bennett straight to them."

"How can she know?" Felix asked, his voice

squealing at the top of its register. "Chris went loopy when Saffron was shot. He might have run off to Kazakhstan again."

"He didn't go loopy," Georgie insisted. "He wanted revenge. And I don't blame him."

"OK, OK. Sorry. Forget about Kazakhstan."

"And they worked together when they were both in NJ7, didn't they? So I reckon she must know where he is and it has to be in London somewhere." Georgie sat back, satisfied that she'd made her point.

"Did you see that one outside the flat this morning?" Felix asked, trying to change the subject.

"The agent you mean?"

"Yeah, the fat one." Felix started laughing. "How did he get into NJ7? He's the size of the moon."

Georgie couldn't help smiling. "It's probably cos he gets no exercise," she chuckled. "He spends his whole life standing outside that flat."

"If he's there when we get home this afternoon, I'm going to take him some cake and a cup of tea."

"Why be so nice to him?"

"You haven't tasted my tea, have you?"

Georgie laughed so hard she nearly choked on the last bite of her apple. When she recovered, she lobbed the core across the hall and ducked down behind her bag. The apple core hit the NJ7 agent right on the shoulder. He jolted to attention and looked around trying to work out where it had come from.

"By the way," said Felix, recovering from a hard bout of giggling, "we should have another codename for you-know-who."

"Who?" Georgie wiped her eyes with the back of her hand.

"You know... her."

"No, I don't know, do I, genius? If I did, I wouldn't have said 'Who?', would I?"

Felix leaned forwards, almost dipping his chest into the remains of his lunch. "Miss Bennett," he mumbled. "From now on let's call her Grandma, OK?"

Georgie put her head in her hands. "You're a nutcase," she sighed. "It doesn't matter about codenames, does it? If they can hear us, we're already finished. And if they can't, then why have any codenames at all? It's ridiculous. Soon we'll have a whole extended family of aunts and uncles and grandmas and great-great-step-nieces when we're not even related to each other."

Felix opened his mouth to protest, but Georgie was already standing up from the table. "Forget it," she said, hooking her bag over her shoulder and waving her hand at Felix to keep him quiet. "I'll see you at home."

25 PROMISES KEPT

Jimmy shivered and scratched at his right shoulder. Behind him, light streamed through a large window covered in lace curtains. It was almost too bright for Jimmy to keep his eyes open. All he wanted to do was find a bed somewhere and crawl into it – preferably somewhere warm with some decent food, but at that moment he wasn't too fussy.

Instead, he was shifting about on an uncomfortable wicker chair, in the front room of a dilapidated two-storey house. He was back in those same old clothes he'd been wearing before he replaced them with the wetsuit. An old hoodie, jeans and some trainers – all stolen from various places on Jimmy's trek between Texas and New York. From the CIA operatives who had brought him here, he gathered that now he was somewhere in the residential heart of Brooklyn. He didn't care. He didn't even know how he felt about surviving the explosion in the North Sea.

He shuddered at the memory of hitting the water. The burning oil on his wetsuit had quickly gone out, but it had left Jimmy with scars all over his body. Every centimetre of his skin itched. He felt like he wanted to rip it off and start again with an entirely new body. Preferably one that was a hundred per cent human.

Every time he closed his eyes, the blackness slowly became an orange glow, with the black silhouette of a man just standing there, waiting. Waiting to die. Jimmy was so confused about Paduk he felt a physical pain in his stomach when he thought about what had happened. It was like two wild dogs were locked in a bloody scrap, but inside his body.

Paduk had saved him, one barked. But only because the man had come back to make sure Jimmy was dead, barked the other. Still, Jimmy had yet another death on his hands to add to the CIA agents killed in the plane crash. But this was different, the other side of him protested. This was the death of an enemy, and what's more, Paduk could have saved himself. He chose not to. Jimmy dropped his head into his hands and tore at his eyes, as if he could physically remove the raging argument from his head. He knew that in death, Paduk had been no enemy.

Why did he need a debrief? The job was done. It had been painful. It had been messy. Paduk had been blown up. That was all that needed to be said. Jimmy's head was throbbing and he thought that if he itched any more, he might throw a fit and tear down the walls. At least his hands had recovered well from the effects of the cold, but that seemed insignificant when stacked up against everything else.

The current had taken Jimmy to the rendezvous on the ship. A CIA doctor had looked him over and done what he could for the burns, but Jimmy didn't think the man had helped much. From there, he'd been flown straight back to New York. And he'd already had enough of the place.

I'm not waiting any more, he thought. He pushed himself up so violently that the chair fell backwards and crashed on the floor. Jimmy didn't know where he would go, just that he needed to get out of there.

Before he reached the door, it swung open and in marched Colonel Keays, in full military uniform as usual, his hat under his arm. Jimmy stopped where he was. He glanced towards the window. There was the shadow of a long black car and Jimmy could hear that the engine was still running.

"Not staying long?" Jimmy asked.

"Sit down," Keays ordered. His voice was stern and the scowl on his face made Jimmy suddenly less sure of himself. "I said sit."

Jimmy shuffled back to his chair. He picked it up slowly and plonked himself down, glaring at Keays.

"Did they make you?" Keays started abruptly.

"What?" Jimmy's eyes stung. Keays knew that NJ7 scientists had designed and built him. Why was he rubbing it in?

"Nobody made me but *me*!" Jimmy yelled. He sat up in his chair, fists clenched.

"Ha!" Keays bellowed, but he still wasn't smiling. "I meant did they see you? It's secret agent talk, kid. I meant did they see you and realise it was you?"

Jimmy sunk back into his chair and felt his muscles relaxing – but only slightly. His blood was still pumping fiercely. "No," he said meekly. "They saw me, but they all thought I was Zafi."

"Uh-huh."

"Except one," Jimmy added. "Paduk." It was the first time he'd said the man's name out loud for a long time. For some reason, it felt awkward on his lips. "He saw me without my mask on, but then he…" Jimmy hesitated.

"He went up like Chinese New Year," Keays cut in. "Ha!" Only now did the hint of a smile bend the corners of his mouth. Jimmy shuddered at the man's coarseness.

"Mitchell was there," Jimmy continued, unable to look Keays in the eye. The memory of the night was too strong. He could feel his muscles twitching and tensing as the images flashed through his mind. "But he called me Zafi. He'll go back to NJ7 and tell them it was her that did it."

"Well at least you did something right," said Keays brashly.

Jimmy felt the man's comment like a paper cut. He wasn't asking for a medal. All he wanted was somebody from the CIA to tell him he'd done a good job.

"I did exactly what you said I should," Jimmy protested. "It was a job you said was almost impossible – and it was. But I did it. Nobody could have any idea that America was involved in this in any way. I risked my life to protect you and your stupid politics."

"No, you did it because if Britain had fired those rockets, your sister and your mother and your little friend Felix would have been blown to pieces by French retaliation."

"OK, who cares? I still did it, didn't I? I got shot at, drowned in oil, blown up and set on fire, but I did it. I destroyed Neptune's Shadow."

"That wasn't your mission."

"*What?*" Jimmy's mind was racing, trying to work out what Colonel Keays could be worried about.

"Who told you to blow up Neptune's Shadow?" Keays went on.

"I couldn't find the missiles," Jimmy grumbled. "They weren't where I thought they would be."

"Then you should have looked a bit harder."

Jimmy bristled with anger. He glared at Keays, not intimidated by the man's rank or power. "Look," he snapped, "what's the difference? The missiles have been destroyed. It's over. What's your problem?"

"My problem is that you were meant to neutralise the base so that I could send in a team to clean up and take over. But you blustered in there and blew the whole damn place to hell! Do you have any idea what the environmental damage is when you detonate a missile base that used to be the world's second-biggest oil rig?"

"Environmental damage?" Jimmy screamed. "You want to see environmental damage?" He pulled his hoodie off over his head and lifted his T-shirt. His stomach was marbled with scarring, red and raw.

Keays scowled and looked away. "OK," he grunted. "I get the picture. What do you want me to do? Cry?"

Jimmy dropped his T-shirt back into place. He felt completely drained of energy. He didn't even see the point of arguing any more. "So what happens now?" he mumbled.

"I promised we'd look after you," Keays replied, "and I plan to keep that promise. The agent outside will escort you to another safehouse for now."

Great, thought Jimmy. *Another safehouse.*

"And after that," Keays went on, "I'll organise another plane to take you out of the country as soon as possible."

Jimmy didn't need to say anything. His expression showed every atom of doubt.

"Don't worry," the colonel reassured him. "I'll make sure everything goes smoothly this time."

Jimmy nodded. What else could he do? He felt completely helpless. He had no choice but to rely completely on Colonel Keays and the CIA, even though they'd already shown how unreliable they were. The last thing Jimmy wanted to do was to have to escape from another nose-diving plane while three more agents were killed for his sake.

Colonel Keays looked hard at Jimmy, up and down. "You'll be fine, Jimmy," he announced, planting his hat on his head. "We got your back."

With that, he marched out of the room. Jimmy overheard a mumbled conversation between him and the agent in the corridor, while outside the car revved its engine.

We got your back, Jimmy repeated in his head, full of scorn. That wasn't the way it had seemed when he'd been out in the North Sea, alone except for an SAS assault team that wanted to kill him.

Jimmy kicked at the dust on the floor. Then, in a burst of rage, he jumped to his feet and hurled his chair at the wall opposite him. It smashed into splinters. Jimmy followed up with his fist. In his belly, his anger locked together with his programming, like two halves of a broken rock. Power surged down Jimmy's arm. His single punch generated a force of nearly 450 kilograms

– as much as a blow from a sledgehammer. And that was the effect it had on the wall.

This wasn't a solid brick outer wall. It was just the flimsy plasterboard between rooms. Flakes of green paint crumbled at Jimmy's feet. Automatically, he rubbed his knuckles, but he didn't care that they were red and hot. He'd made a hole in the wall about the size of a tennis ball, giving him a view straight through into the back room of the house. It was as bare as the room Jimmy was standing in. His eyes fixed on the back window. His breath froze in his throat.

Lace curtains covered the glass, just like in the front room, but at one end was a sliver that they didn't quite reach. Jimmy had a glimpse of what was happening in the back alley behind the house. There was a long black car waiting out there, just like the one at the front. And inside it was a ghost. That was the only explanation Jimmy could think of. Sitting in the front passenger seat, hunched down on the black leather, was a man with dark skin and a fresh scar under his eye.

Jimmy looked harder. He swayed his head to try and get a view from every possible perspective. Then the car pulled away. The man was gone. But Jimmy had only needed a second to know exactly who it was. Into Jimmy's mind flashed the man's face as it had been the last time he had seen it, with that spike of glass sticking into his cheek just below his eye. The man's dying cry was seared into Jimmy's memory.

Except the man wasn't dead. He was in Brooklyn. Now. Jimmy had seen him. He was certain that he had just seen Agent Bligh.

26 CHASING GHOSTS

Jimmy rushed out of the room into the hallway. The world seemed to sway in front of him as he moved. Was he seeing things that weren't real? How could Bligh still be alive? Jimmy had seen the man being blown out of a plane hundreds of metres up in the sky. Jimmy had been the only one with a parachute to himself and the chance to open it. Froy and Bligh had died. But now it was as if the plane crash hadn't really happened at all. Jimmy was terrified that he was losing his mind.

"It was him!" he panted. Keays had already left, but the other CIA agent was there – the one who'd brought Jimmy to Brooklyn. "Bligh! Bligh's alive!"

Confusion shot across the agent's face. He was another tall, lean man – like every one of the American agents Jimmy had encountered. This one had grey hair and fat drooping lips that made him look like some kind of trout.

"Bligh's dead," he grunted, shrugging. He had a thick New York accent. "Fell outta plane." There was no emotion in his voice, but loud smacking noises as he chewed on some gum.

"You don't understand," Jimmy protested. "I just saw him. At the back of this building, in a car. You're working with him on this, aren't you?"

The agent's eyes flicked over Jimmy's head for a second. He saw the damage Jimmy had done to the wall. "Forget it," he said. "You're upset. Trauma, probably. Let's get out of here."

He marched into the street and held open the back door of the long black car. Jimmy gazed into the street. Everything seemed so calm. Then he caught a glimpse of the back of a car disappearing round a corner. Was that Bligh's sedan? It could have been any car in the world, but in Jimmy's head it created a storm of bewilderment.

Didn't the CIA know Bligh was still alive? If Bligh wasn't here as part of the CIA unit, then what was he doing here?

He's here for me, Jimmy thought. Fear jabbed his stomach. Why else had the man been waiting behind a random house in Brooklyn? Could Bligh be working for NJ7? It sounded ridiculous, but so did the idea that Bligh had survived the plane crash.

In the back of Jimmy's mind he could sense vague

calculations going on. His programming was working out which kinds of portable listening device could be used to pick up conversation inside a house, what their range was, how much could have been heard or even recorded... It was a jumble of frenetic thoughts with only one conclusion. Bligh must have been listening to Jimmy's conversation with Keays. Jimmy knew it. But why? Who was he working for? Jimmy had to find him.

He shuffled out to the car, still dazed. He could feel himself shaking as he took his seat in the back. The door slammed shut and his escort slipped into the front passenger seat, next to the driver.

"Listen," pleaded Jimmy, "if you don't know about Bligh, he's fooling you all. I saw him. He's alive."

"You gotta relax," said the agent. "Get over your emotions. You're seeing dead men."

Jimmy clenched his fists, all the time thinking frantically. "No!" he insisted. "You have to tell Keays. Radio him now or something. Tell him Bligh survived the crash." Jimmy's voice kept rising, full of panic. "Tell him Bligh's working for NJ7! And he's here! He's in Brooklyn!"

The agents in the front glanced at each other and tutted. Jimmy slumped back in his seat, feeling his heart punching at his ribcage.

The car pulled away. *We're going the wrong way*, shouted a voice in Jimmy's head. Bligh's car had headed in the opposite direction. Jimmy swivelled on the leather as they turned into the main street. He watched the shop fronts glide past, putting more and more distance between him and Bligh.

"You OK back there?" asked the driver after a moment of silence.

"Yeah," said Jimmy in a low voice. "Emotions. Must be the trauma."

The driver and the other agent exchanged another glance.

"Hey," Jimmy called out quickly. "I'm hungry. Stop the car here." Jimmy pointed at one of the stores. "I'll get bagels. What kind do you want?"

The driver looked at Jimmy suspiciously in the rear-view mirror. "What's he gonna do?" muttered the other agent. "Strangle you with a bagel?"

The driver shrugged and pulled up at the next corner. Jimmy was about to jump out, but stopped himself. "I'll need some money," he announced, holding out a hand.

"Stay here," the agent answered, warily. "If you want a bagel, I'll get it for you." He pulled out a wallet and inspected it to see how much money he had. "You want anything?" he muttered to the driver.

The driver shrugged. "Coffee," he said.

The agent sighed and reached for the door handle. Jimmy was so quick the man only realised what was happening after it was over. Jimmy snatched the wallet with his left hand and at the same time opened the car door with his right.

"Hey!" the agent yelled.

Jimmy was already belting round the corner. The car screeched after him, one door still flapping open.

"Radio Keays and follow me!" Jimmy yelled, bursting into the nearest store, an Internet café. He vaulted over the counter. Everybody in the café screamed. Jimmy was already crashing his way through the back of the store. He smashed out of the fire escape, never dropping his pace.

Meanwhile, his mind was aching. He'd seen which direction Bligh was travelling – but only at first. How many times could he have changed direction since then? Jimmy had to work out Bligh's approximate position based on his original direction and probable speed. If he did, then he could catch up by running in a dead straight line, diagonally across the roads and through any buildings that stood in his way.

He burst into a drugstore and was gone out of the back exit before anybody in there could draw breath. His instincts guided him, forcing his body to move just as it needed to. He pumped his legs with fierce power and regularity.

He reached the main road. Ahead of him, the massive arcs of Brooklyn Bridge rose into the sky like a gothic monument. Traffic trundled past, joining the end of a jam.

Jimmy pulled to a halt and scanned the cars. Manoeuvring into the outside lane was a long black sedan.

Jimmy glanced behind him and waited a split-second. Any moment he expected his CIA escort to catch up. If Jimmy led them straight to Bligh, they would have to do something about it. He dashed into the line of cars, waving his arms above his head. To a hail of beeps and honks, Jimmy yanked open the door of a yellow cab.

"Follow that car," Jimmy ordered, his voice quiet but firm.

The driver almost choked. "You serious?" he asked. His face was heavily lined, a medley of every shade of brown. Jimmy gave him a commanding stare. "OK," shrugged the driver, with an accent that wasn't American, but Jimmy couldn't quite place it.

The road in front of them was dense with cars. Bligh's sedan wove from lane to lane, making slow but persistent progress over the bridge. On the other side it was hard to even get a clear view of Bligh's car through the jumble of trucks and street signs.

"He's there!" Jimmy yelled. "There! He's indicating left."

"I see it, I see it," the cab driver insisted.

"So don't lose him!"

"Where you from?" the driver asked, peeking at Jimmy in the mirror.

"Who cares where I'm from?" Jimmy snapped. He could see the back end of Bligh's car disappearing round a corner in Manhattan's Tribeca district. There were six or seven cars between them now. Jimmy twitched nervously. "Come on!" he urged between his teeth.

"You Australian?" the driver asked.

"Just drive!" Jimmy yelled.

The driver tutted. "Where can I go?" He waved a hand in front of him at the solid wall of cars in the way. "Australians. Always impatient."

That was it. Jimmy had had enough. If he lost Bligh now, the man would disappear. Jimmy rattled on the door. It was locked.

"Let me out!" he shouted. His head was fuming. The driver shrugged again and pressed a couple of buttons on the meter. He slowly shifted the taxi to the side of the road and announced a price to Jimmy. Jimmy wasn't even listening. The driver did everything so slowly Jimmy was tempted to punch through the perspex screen between them and rip the man's head off.

Take control, he told himself. *Calm down.* He thrust a fistful of dollar bills through the hatch to the driver and burst out on to the street. He hurtled past the traffic and round the corner. There was no sign of Bligh. Jimmy kept running. That car had to have gone somewhere. At the next crossroads Jimmy looked in every direction.

The intersection of West 18th Street and 6th Avenue was bustling with people, cars, roadworks –

everything except the car he was looking for.

"No!" Jimmy cried out. He bent double and pounded his fists on his knees. "I saw him! He was there!"

He tried to think everything through rationally, but he could feel paranoia creeping across the burns on his skin. If Bligh was working for someone else, what if those other CIA agents were as well? That's the only reason Jimmy could think of why they would be so reluctant to radio Colonel Keays. Jimmy gasped as the facts slowly clicked into place in his head. The agents who were chasing him hadn't called for back-up. Why?

Any second they would catch up with him. Until now, that's what Jimmy had planned – he'd wanted to lead them to Bligh. But the foundation of Jimmy's trust in them had crumbled.

That's when he decided to find Bligh on his own.

Suddenly, Jimmy felt a prickle chase through him. The hairs stood up on his arms and on the back of his neck. He ran his eyes up the skyscraper directly opposite. It was a massive building, all sleek black glass. It stood on the corner of the block, with a small courtyard at the entrance. *What am I looking for?* Jimmy thought to himself. Something about the building seemed magnetic.

That's when Jimmy saw it. At the top of the tower was a huge logo: a fat black 'S' on a grey disc. A wisp of cloud floated past and made it seem like the ground was spinning. Jimmy felt dizzy and looked back to the entrance of the building. Just above the entrance, and below a flagpole carrying a huge stars and stripes flag, was the logo again.

It was the same black S that Jimmy had seen on the side of the *Risavottur*. He thought back to what Captain Peck had told him. It had seemed harmless at the time – they'd borrowed an oil tanker from a small US oil company called…

Jimmy searched for the name. Syn-something… He closed his eyes and could taste the salt of the North Sea. Then it hit him. His programming screamed it at him – Synperco. Had Bligh gone into this building? Why? Who were Synperco? And why had a dead CIA agent come straight to their offices after spying on Jimmy?

There was only one way to find out.

27 SPIT AND DUST

Jimmy crossed over to the Synperco building, but he steered clear of the front courtyard. He didn't want to be picked up on their security cameras. He kept his head down and didn't even look through the glass frontage into the lobby. Instead, he glanced at the reflection in the window of a parked car.

In a second, he'd established the number of security guards and their positions. There were too many of them. Then there was also the electronic surveillance and the security measures on the doors and elevators. There was no way Jimmy would be able to infiltrate the building through the lobby.

Slowly, Jimmy moved on and round the corner. The street was packed with people – mainly men and women in suits, bustling along with their briefcases. For a moment, Jimmy doubted himself. With all these people around it was perfectly possible that Bligh had just disappeared in the crowd. Could it be a coincidence that Jimmy had lost him outside the Synperco building?

Jimmy felt that doubt scratching at his insides. It was as annoying as the itching of his burns. *No*, he told himself. *It's too much of a coincidence.* Even if he couldn't find Bligh, somewhere in this building must lie answers to what the man had been doing.

Further along was an entrance to the underground parking. There was a booth, manned by a security guard, along with more cameras and a double barrier to stop unauthorised cars getting in.

A Cadillac swooped round the corner and flashed its indicator. It was about to turn into the underground parking lot. Jimmy felt a thump in his chest. It was his programming kicking into action. The car slowed to make the turn and the driver's window rolled down.

This is your chance, Jimmy shouted inside his head. *Move!* But his programming held his muscles in check until the perfect moment. Just as the security guard glanced at the driver's ID card, Jimmy dropped to the ground and rolled under the car. He locked his fingers on to the undercarriage. The car never stopped completely, but when the barrier was raised to let it pass, Jimmy was attached to it.

Dust caught in his throat and swirled into his eyes. The backs of his heels dragged down the concrete ramp under him, but he held on. The sunlight grew distant and was replaced by the strip lights of the parking lot. Jimmy coughed and spluttered in the Cadillac's grime. It was hot too – like slowly roasting in an oven. But it was nothing compared to some of the trials Jimmy had been through lately.

I should be used to this by now, he thought. He had thrown himself underneath cars several times already, acting on the impulse from his programming, but he still didn't think it would ever feel like a natural way to travel.

He waited for the car to pull into a space, then dropped to the ground. He rolled out from under the car while the engine was still running and lay on his front under the next car along. He wanted to see where the driver went when he got out.

A man's polished shoes appeared and marched across the asphalt. The echo hammered on Jimmy's nerves. He couldn't stop his mind flashing back to the first night that NJ7 had come for him. He'd hidden under his family's car then, while the agents took away his parents.

For this single moment, Jimmy wished he could turn off his memories or wipe them from his brain. His programming had no memories. It had systems. Whatever situation he was in, his programming reacted. It was reliable. Consistent. Sometimes it was tested, but at least Jimmy knew that the assassin inside him would respond to any crisis with mathematical precision and a complete lack of emotion. Humans weren't so trustworthy.

Jimmy spat out a mouthful of grime. The globule congealed on the concrete. *My DNA is in that*, Jimmy thought. He imagined an NJ7 scientist reconstructing another one of him from the DNA in this sample of saliva. Would he turn out the same way? What if they made two of him? Or a whole army?

Before his thoughts could run away, the Cadillac driver disappeared through a door on the other side of the parking lot. Jimmy sprang into action. Crouching all the time so that he was hidden by the cars, he scurried to the door and pulled it open. He found himself looking at a bank of five lifts.

With the push of a single button, he could make it inside Synperco. But which button? The next lift was ready to go. The doors were open, inviting Jimmy in, but on the wall of the lift was a grid of over a hundred buttons. He could pick a floor at random, but what good would that do him? It was a huge skyscraper. It would take him forever to search every room on every floor. And he didn't even know what he was looking for.

He could feel the battle going on inside him – the frustration of the human boy and the calm scheming of the assassin. He knew that with every passing second, the human was being squeezed out.

Instead of jumping into the lift and wandering about

the building, Jimmy edged back into the parking lot. He crouched again and moved through the lines of cars, winding his way through. What was he looking for? He could feel his programming humming inside him.

It took him a couple of minutes to realise what his subconscious had sent him to find. And then he saw it – Bligh's car. The long black sedan was nestled in line, like a panther in the traps at a greyhound race.

Jimmy sidled up to it. Then suddenly, his foot kicked out at the next car along. Jimmy thought he had developed a spasm, but realised he'd loosened the hubcap of the car next to the sedan. He reached down and snapped off the plastic cover. *What am I doing?* he thought. His disbelief rose a second later when he reached into the workings of the wheel and scraped his fingers along the edge of the brake.

He pulled his hand back. His fingers were coated in a densely-packed layer of brake dust. *Vandalising the car won't do any good*, he told himself. But then, very carefully, he opened his palm just next to the handle of the sedan's passenger door and blew.

A cloud of brake dust puffed up, covering the door handle. Only now did Jimmy begin to understand what he was doing – but he still couldn't work out how it would help. He reached up to his head and pinched a few hairs. His hair was greasy and tangled. In some places the tips were still yellow from where he'd bleached it, but that was hardly visible after so many different disguises. Only the very roots showed Jimmy's natural sandy brown.

He tugged sharply, almost surprising himself. It brought water to his eyes, but he didn't let the slight discomfort trouble him. Then, using his hairs as a brush, he gently swept off the excess brake dust. It left a black smear across the car's silver trim.

Jimmy stared at the smudge. *This is ridiculous*, he thought. But then he felt the muscles in his eyes growing tense and his brain whirring. He moved his head even closer, until his nose was almost touching the car door. Gradually, he could make out lines within the dust – swirling shapes, like a labyrinth. Where the lines twisted, his brain seemed to put some kind of marker, like a pin on a map. What had started out as a daub of black muck had transformed into a perfect fingerprint.

Would he even have been able to see it without his programming? He didn't know, but he couldn't wait around to study it any more. He dashed back to the lifts, still cradling some brake dust in his hand and keeping his head below the level of the car roofs.

He felt the muscles in his neck lock. He knew he was on camera. *Just don't look up*, he told himself, though his body would never have let him even if he'd wanted to. He called the lifts and the first set of doors pinged open. Jimmy stepped in.

Working quickly, Jimmy blew more brake dust over the shimmering brass panel of buttons. These lifts were clearly kept in immaculate condition. The mirrors on the walls gleamed. Everything must have been freshly polished that morning and Jimmy guessed that nobody had used that particular lift that day except the cleaner.

He brushed down the buttons with his strands of hair. All that was left was a single thumbprint. Jimmy dismissed it as an obvious mismatch. The shape of the swirl was completely wrong.

In the next lift, there was more to do. The buttons became a medley of blackened smudges where the grease on people's fingers had shown up in the dust. Prints were layered on top of each other, each one clamouring for priority. Jimmy's temples were throbbing. He couldn't take his eyes off the buttons and had to stick his foot out to stop the doors closing.

With so much information to analyse, he couldn't be sure what he was seeing. It was hard enough to keep in his head the shape and contour points of the print that he was looking for. It was the most complicated game of snap he could have imagined.

He turned to the next lift. Clangs echoed through to him from the parking lot. At any second somebody could arrive to interrupt Jimmy's work. He was almost out of brake dust and his spirits were falling. What had seemed so ridiculous to him at first, and then so clever, was now the most idiotic plan anybody could have suggested to him. He dusted his hands clean and raised his fist, ready to punch the buttons. He didn't care where the lift was going to take him any more. He didn't even know why he'd bothered sneaking into the building.

But he stopped himself. There it was, on button 57. Gleaming like a black diamond in a rock was a fragment of a print that matched the image in Jimmy's head. He closed his eyes to double-check his memory, teasing out every detail of the print he'd seen on the door of the sedan. When he opened his eyes, there was its twin.

"Hello, Bligh," he muttered with a smile.

28 FLOOR 57

Jimmy watched the numbers above the door illuminate as the lift passed each floor. At the same time, he could feel the scrutiny of the security cameras on him. There was no camera visible, but that just made it worse – it meant they were hidden behind the mirrors at eye level. Simply keeping his head down was no good.

Jimmy could almost hear the rumblings of the security database running an ID check on his face. But it wouldn't be necessary. Anyone casually glancing at the footage would know that he wasn't meant to be there. First, he wasn't wearing a security pass, and second, how many oil companies employed twelve-year-old boys?

Jimmy was alone until the fourteenth floor, when the lift stopped to let on a clutch of businesspeople. They all gave him funny looks, but none of them said anything. Jimmy avoided eye contact and gave an anonymous smile. Inside, his heart was thumping.

Within a minute, these people would alert security personally.

The twentieth floor flashed past. At twenty-five, some people were let off and a fresh batch of suits got on. Again, they all gave Jimmy a thorough looking over. Thirty floors up and still nobody had challenged him. But he knew that security would be coming for him now.

If they knew who he was – and what he was – they would come hard. But if security thought he was just an ordinary kid who had sneaked into the building somehow, or the son of an employee who had got himself lost, then Jimmy would have the upper hand.

At the thirty-fifth floor, everybody got out of the lift except Jimmy and a middle-aged man in a grey pinstripe suit. The doors slid towards each other. Then, at the last possible instant, a hand reached in and forced them open again. Jimmy felt his muscles flicker as if an electric current had passed right through him. The man stepping into the lift was tall and wiry, with a thin beard. He was dressed in a light blue suit that didn't fit him properly and on his chest was a silver badge. Without even looking up, Jimmy could make out the bulge in his jacket and knew there was a gun on the man's hip.

The man looked straight at Jimmy and his eyes took on a grey stare. The doors closed behind him and the lift carried on towards the fifty-seventh floor. The man's gaze didn't waver.

"How you doin', kid?" he asked in a thick New York accent.

Jimmy still refused to look at him directly. He was silently counting off the floors, waiting for the right moment to make his move. 37, 38, 39... He could feel his limbs were locked in position, but the muscles were growing warm. His body was ready. *Only two casualties*, he heard in his head. *Easy targets. Disarm the guard. Shoot both men.* He clenched his fists, desperate to force out those lethal thoughts.

42, 43, 44... Sweat dripped down the back of his neck. He squeezed his eyes shut. But now he could picture even more clearly the swift and deadly fight his assassin instinct demanded: *One kick to deflect the guard's hands. Swivel into the man's midriff. Use the weapon while it's still in the holster. BANG!* Jimmy flinched and opened his eyes.

"You OK?" the guard asked, leaning towards Jimmy. "You lost?"

Jimmy could hardly hear him. He wanted to scream at the guard to stay back, but was terrified that if he relaxed his muscles enough to speak, his programming would swoop on the gun. *BANG! BANG!* Jimmy flinched again at the sounds in his head. They seemed too real. He even heard the double thump of the two bodies hitting the carpet.

49, 50, 51... Jimmy told himself to focus on the

numbers. He stood rigid. Every twitch in every sinew was magnified a thousand times to him. Each one could be the first act of a mini-bloodbath. The mirrors on the walls seemed to rise up and push Jimmy down. It was as if they were reflecting his true self, and crushing his weak human resistance.

53, 54, 55... Jimmy felt like his heart was crumpling. But he had to hold on. He had to keep the fight inside him. He couldn't let it explode into the outside world, which would surely leave these two men dead.

Finally, Jimmy lifted his right arm. It moved slowly and even he couldn't be sure what he was going to do. The lift slid smoothly to a standstill. The doors opened. Jimmy forced his lips to move.

"Come on, Dad." The words came out of his mouth in a Brooklyn accent. He grabbed the man in the pinstripe suit by the wrist and marched out of the lift. The man was startled. He tried to pull his arm away and shake Jimmy off, but Jimmy was gripping so tightly it was impossible. Jimmy led the man quickly away from the lift.

"What the hell...?" the businessman yelled. Jimmy cut him off.

"Sorry, Dad," he replied loudly. The man dropped his briefcase and tried to prise Jimmy's fingers apart. Jimmy glanced over his shoulder. The lift doors were sliding closed. Was the security guard still watching? Jimmy had only made it a couple of metres away.

There was nowhere else to go. In front of them was a locked door, with a slider for a security pass next to it.

Jimmy waited one more heartbeat, until he heard the lift doors seal behind him.

"Open the door," Jimmy ordered, his fingers digging into the man's wrist.

"Who are you?"

Jimmy glared at him and gripped even harder. "Open the door!" he insisted. Now the man's face changed – from confusion to anger.

"I can't," he replied. "My pass doesn't work on this floor. Now are you gonna let me go or not?"

Jimmy dropped the man's wrist. "Sorry," he mumbled. Then, in one smooth action, the man reached into his jacket pocket and pulled out a swipe card. He swished it through the reader and slipped through the door in a flash, pushing it sharply shut behind him. He gave Jimmy a smug smile through the pane of safety glass.

Jimmy's mouth dropped open, but he didn't panic. He knew that if he needed to he could break through the door into the office space. But he didn't want to. He could hear the businessman running through the corridors shouting for security. In under a minute, there would be guards crawling over this floor.

Fortunately, it was the wrong floor. Knowing that in the lift he wouldn't be able to avoid the security cameras, Jimmy had pressed the button marked 56 –

not 57. Now all he needed to do was get up one floor without being spotted by a person or a camera.

He glanced around him. The bare white landing area had only the five lifts and this single door. Access through it was by swipe card. There was no other way out – the emergency stairs were evidently somewhere else in the building. And there was only a single camera, in the corner above the door.

Jimmy started kicking at the door, as if he was trying to break it down. Actually, he was putting on a show for the camera. He deliberately held his strength in check. With his next kick he pretended that he'd hurt his foot. He fixed a grimace on his face and hopped around, clutching his foot. Finally, he dropped to the floor and pulled off his trainer. He hoped that whoever was keeping an eye on the security footage was having a laugh at his expense. But they were about to get a shock.

Jimmy stood up suddenly and pretended he was about to charge at the door. He set off at a run, hurling his shoe into the air. It struck the security camera at the perfect angle, knocking it a fraction to one side. Jimmy diverted his run at the last second and darted to the lift at the end of the row, picking up his shoe on the way.

If he'd done this right, the camera would now have a blind spot – and Jimmy was in it. He shoved his foot back into his trainer, which took an extra second because it was slightly too small.

He jumped and caught the lip above the lift doors. He pulled himself up. He could feel the vibrations of the lift rumbling towards him. How many guards had they sent? He clambered up the wall until he could reach the ceiling, balanced with the tips of his toes digging in where his fingers had just been.

A ceiling panel came loose with a sharp tap. Jimmy hauled himself up into a crawlspace. He pulled himself forwards on his elbows, carefully judging how far he had to go to tunnel under the security door. Then he punched his way through the panel over his head to the floor above, ripping a hole in the carpet.

His positioning was perfect. *Who needs a swipe card*, he thought, dusting off his clothes. He kicked the floor panel back into place and smoothed down the carpet with his foot.

In front of him was a long corridor with offices on either side. Each office had a large window into the corridor, but fortunately nobody had witnessed Jimmy's little reconstruction job. Everybody had their head down, engrossed in a pile of papers or a computer screen.

He knew he was on camera again now. There was nothing he could do about that. But as long as security were still looking for him on the floor below, he could get away with it if he moved fast.

Jimmy travelled briskly through the offices. How long would it take security to do a thorough sweep of the floor below? How long before they double-checked the surveillance footage and saw where Jimmy really was? He had no idea. He peered into every office. They all looked the same – a window, a wall covered by filing cabinets, another with reference books and a large wooden desk with a computer on it. Some rooms were slightly larger, and some seemed to have more piles of papers all over the place or a couple of pot plants, but nothing stood out.

What was Jimmy after? *I've lost my mind*, he thought to himself. *I've just smashed my way into the fifty-seventh floor of an office block and I've no idea what I'm looking for.*

He hunched his shoulders, refocusing on what he had to do: find Bligh. *I didn't imagine him,* Jimmy told himself. *I found his car. I took his fingerprint.* But really he knew all that meant nothing – a black car and a fingerprint leading him to the fifty-seventh floor might have had nothing to do with Agent Bligh. Maybe Bligh really was at the bottom of the ocean. Jimmy could picture the man's strange serenity as he was sucked from the aeroplane and the glass sticking out of his cheek.

Jimmy gritted his teeth and told himself over and over, *He's alive. He's here.* Somehow, Jimmy was convinced of it: a CIA agent had survived a lethal plane crash, then come back to New York to spy on him. But he had no idea *why*.

29 THE ILLUSION OF POISON

Jimmy hurried on through the building. Until now he'd had no idea how much office space there could be on a single floor of a massive skyscraper. The corridors seemed to go on forever, just like the bunkers of NJ7 headquarters in London. Except here it was quiet, with bright light and coarse blue carpet, instead of echoing hallways and concrete breeze blocks. Despite the difference, the air was just as stifling.

Jimmy rounded the next corner, ducking below the level of the office windows that looked on to the corridor. Suddenly, Jimmy's eyes flashed wider. The next office had its Venetian blind down, but not fully closed. Through the slats, Jimmy could see a man hunched over his desk, engrossed in whatever was on his laptop.

He was silhouetted against the backdrop of his office window, with a stunning view all the way down 6th Avenue to New York's financial district. Only the light from his computer caught his face. He had curly black hair, dark skin and a fresh scar on his cheek, just below one eye. Jimmy's heart picked up pace and his veins seemed to buzz with the power of his programming. He'd found Bligh.

Jimmy's first instinct was to burst into the office and confront the man. But what would he learn in a fight? The assassin in Jimmy was already working on an alternative. At the end of the corridor was a water cooler and the doors to the bathrooms. Jimmy scurried there now, staying bent over so he couldn't be seen from inside the offices.

A bead of sweat dropped from Lex Bligh's forehead and plopped on to his keyboard. He swore under his breath and leaned back in his chair. There was no way he could concentrate on his work when it was so hot. In the last few minutes, the internal climate system had gone haywire, and on the fifty-seventh floor of a skyscraper you can't just open a window for a bit of fresh air.

He phoned down to the maintenance department. They promised to take a look at it before the end of the day. *I'll have melted by then*, Bligh thought, slamming the phone down. He pushed off from his desk, wheeling backwards on his chair half a metre. He mopped his face with his tie and jumped up to fetch a glass of water from the cooler in the corridor.

He had gulped down three cupfuls before he noticed the strange taste. He wiped his lips and, like a fool, took another cup to try and take the taste away. He dropped his head all the way back and poured it down. It was as the last drop trickled down his throat that he noticed the shelf high above the water cooler. A bottle of bleach was lying open, on its side – and empty. For a second, all Bligh could see was the bright warning sign on the bottle: HIGHLY TOXIC. KEEP OUT OF REACH OF CHILDREN.

Bligh doubled up, coughing. He staggered forwards, steadying himself on the water cooler. It toppled over, sending a cascade of water down the corridor. Bligh hauled himself into the bathroom.

Jimmy was already in Bligh's office, rifling through the filing cabinets. His fingers moved at astonishing speed. On his face was an expression of calm concentration. He had no concerns for Bligh's health. All Jimmy had done was put a few drops of ordinary soap in the water – enough to ensure that Bligh would spot the taste after a couple of cups, but nothing that would be at all poisonous. Then Jimmy had broken into the cleaner's cupboard, taken the bleach bottle and emptied the contents down the toilet. He'd placed the empty bottle on the shelf above the water cooler.

The hardest thing had been deciding the bottle's exact position, making sure that Bligh would see it and jump to the obvious conclusion. Jimmy had discovered instinctively what all assassins know – sometimes making someone think you've harmed them is more powerful than actually harming them.

Jimmy wiped his face with his sleeve. He was dripping with sweat. The last part of his scheme to get Bligh out of his office had been the easiest. Above the ceiling panels in the corridor was the electrical wiring. A single cable powered the thermostat that controlled the temperature in Bligh's office. Jimmy had easily recalibrated it. It would have been impossible to stay in that room for more than a few minutes without needing a glass of water.

Now Jimmy had to hope that Bligh would be stuck in the bathroom long enough for Jimmy to find something – anything. He started with the filing cabinets, but they weren't locked. Immediately, he suspected that what they contained would be useless. And he was right.

He pulled out fistfuls of glossy Synperco brochures and company reports and flicked through them. They blathered on for pages and pages about plans for expansion and charts of financial projections. It was gibberish to Jimmy. Then there were a couple of pictures – the opening of a new oil rig and the launching of a new tanker. Jimmy studied them, but didn't recognise any of the names or faces. If any of it was encrypted information, it was too well disguised for Jimmy to identify.

He glanced through the glass between the slats, into the corridor. If Bligh came back, Jimmy would have no warning. He quickly tugged the cord on the blind to close the slats. Now he could at least carry on his work without being observed. In his head was the constant calculation – how many paces from the bathroom to the office? How long would Bligh take before he either worked out he hadn't been poisoned or puked up all the contents of his stomach?

Jimmy's mind was racing. By now, his doubt about Bligh had taken firm hold. The man surely wasn't still working for the CIA – if he ever really had. He might have been working for Synperco all along, and been placed with the CIA as a double agent. He could have been uncovering CIA secrets and passing them back to Synperco. Perhaps, after surviving the attack on the plane, he'd deliberately made everyone think he was dead to escape being caught by the CIA...

Stop, Jimmy ordered himself. His imagination was running away. What would a small US oil company want with CIA intelligence? And if Bligh had used NJ7's attack to pretend to be dead, why would he come back to spy on Jimmy? It made no sense. It was more likely that

Bligh was working for NJ7. The thought chilled Jimmy's bones. But if it was true, where did Synperco fit in?

Jimmy abandoned the filing cabinet and turned instead to Bligh's desk. This was much more promising. Jimmy slipped into the soft leather chair and picked his way through the papers on the desk, being careful not to dislodge anything. As far as he could see, they were all financial documents. Long lists of huge figures in tiny print, with only initials to indicate what they meant. Jimmy had no way of knowing what the initials stood for.

He let out a huff in exasperation. Then he froze. Were there footsteps in the corridor? The sound passed. Jimmy breathed again and redoubled his efforts. Any second, Bligh could be back or, worse, the building's security team could be on to him.

Jimmy expertly clicked through the folders on Bligh's laptop. This didn't take any special assassin skills – it was the same operating system Jimmy had used for years at home. Bligh had left one document open. It had the word 'Director' in bold, then a long string of numbers and the word 'Flight'. To Jimmy it meant nothing. It must have been some kind of private flight schedule, but Jimmy had no interest in travel arrangements or holiday plans. He dismissed it and moved on to the list of recently opened documents.

The file names were all encrypted. Each one was a

series of five capital letters. For a few seconds, Jimmy puzzled over names like XPTYU and PGIWV. It was useless. There was no way he could work out what they meant in his head, and when he tried to open them, the computer asked for a password.

Jimmy slammed his fist on the desk. His hands were so sweaty now that he was having trouble controlling the cursor. But then at last he saw a flaw in the security. While the individual file names were encrypted, the folders they were organised in didn't seem to be. And one in particular caught Jimmy's eye: NEP.SHA.

Tantalisingly slowly, Jimmy felt his brain making connections. But there was too much he didn't know. It was like trying to build a house of cards in the dark.

NEP.SHA. NEP.SHA. Jimmy repeated it to himself over and over. It had to mean Neptune's Shadow. He felt a rush of excitement, mixed with a flash of terror from his night in the North Sea. He told himself to calm down and piece it together bit by bit: he was in the offices of an oil company. Before it had blown up, Neptune's Shadow had been the world's second-largest oil rig. Now this folder, called NEP.SHA – it was obviously all connected. But how? Then Jimmy remembered one more thing – the man whose computer he was on was the man who had originally told him about Neptune's Shadow.

"Come on," Jimmy whispered. "Think!"

He held his head in his hands, desperately trying to work out what was going on. But all he came up with was a headache. He'd never been very good at solving puzzles or riddles. He didn't have the patience. He remembered his father always telling him to think "around the problem", but Jimmy didn't really know what that meant. He shoved that memory aside. The last thing he needed was a reminder of Ian Coates pretending to be his father for all those years.

To distract himself he opened the Internet browser and Googled "Neptune's Shadow". There were hundreds of thousands of pages all about the oil industry. Jimmy scrolled through them, letting his vision blur. It was useless. He wasn't used to so many results coming up for a search term – in Britain search results were censored. He tried Googling "NEP.SHA", but this time only one page came up and it was in Finnish. Jimmy didn't have time to see whether he could understand it.

It looked like the only people who could tell him anything new about Neptune's Shadow were the CIA and Synperco. His mind was rolling round in circles. He had already been sitting in that office far too long. He didn't have time to solve puzzles. He needed information.

Ask NJ7, he heard in his head. It came at him out of the blue, almost making him jump with shock. This time it wasn't his programming. It was the sudden realisation that somebody else *did* know about Neptune's Shadow, apart from the CIA and Synperco – the British Secret Service.

Suddenly, Jimmy realised what an incredible opportunity he had. For the first time since arriving in America he had access to the Internet. The other thing he had was a friend inside NJ7 who might be able to give him information to explain what was going on. In the next few seconds, before security or Bligh came charging through that door, Jimmy had to find a way to communicate with Eva.

He perched on the edge of his seat, his knee bouncing up and down. His hands were like vultures' claws hovering over the keyboard. But he didn't know what to do. He obviously couldn't email. Even if his old email address still worked, the second he logged in, he would be telling NJ7 that he was still alive. And, for that matter, he didn't know Eva's email address – eva@NJ7.co.uk? He shook his head and told himself not to be so ridiculous.

So his only option was to leave a message somewhere on a forum or in a chatroom. But there were billions of them and Jimmy had time to leave a message in only one. He'd done this before. When he'd wanted Georgie and Felix to come and join him in London, he'd trawled every site he could think of where his sister might stumble across a message by chance. It had worked – but Jimmy still didn't know which one site she had found the message on.

Suddenly, he felt a shiver. He may not know how to get in touch with them, but they had already sent a message to him.

Jimmy reached to the back pocket of his jeans. It was still there – the scrap of paper that his sister and his friend had scribbled "Happy Birthday" on. Jimmy smoothed it out on the desk. This had to be the key. It was more than just a birthday greeting. They were trying to tell him something.

But before Jimmy could study the message, his time ran out. The door of the office creaked open.

30 A LITTLE WAR

Jimmy jumped to his feet. He slammed the laptop shut, tucked it under his arm and grabbed his birthday message with his other hand. Then he climbed straight over the desk and hurtled towards the office door. He moved so fast it looked like the door was opening in slow motion. The security guard coming in had no time to adjust for what was about to hit him.

Jimmy dropped his shoulder and blasted into the man's midriff. The guard doubled up and slumped to the carpet. But the rest of the corridor was packed with armed security agents. Jimmy kept his head down and dived for the glimmers of light between the uniforms, squeezing through their grasps.

He hurtled down the corridor. The thunder of feet chasing him was a familiar noise by now and it didn't put him off. Neither did the frantic shouts for him to stop or the crackle of walkie-talkies. A single glance at a sign on the wall told him exactly where to go – it was the map of the floor with the evacuation route highlighted. The arrows fixed in Jimmy's head and guided him through the building to an emergency exit. He smashed through the door and found himself in a stairwell.

He stuck his head out over the rail. Beneath him was a fifty-six-floor spiral. It seemed to go on forever. Running down was pointless. By the time he'd gone even halfway, there would be an army of security forces, probably including his CIA escort, waiting for him at the bottom.

Instead, Jimmy spun on his heels and charged upwards. His running was regular – two steps at a time, never one and never three. The smack of his feet on the concrete stairs was like a drum machine.

He had to squeeze his arm close to his side to keep hold of the laptop, but he didn't let it slow him down. In his other hand he held up the scrap of paper with the note from Georgie and Felix. His eyes jumped straight to the bottom, where part of Felix's message read, "...your sister's given some good advice so do what she says".

Advice? Jimmy thought. He quickly scanned what Georgie had written, just above Felix's scrawl:

Happy Birthday! Sorry u don't have a present from me. I'd get a book or something, but I don't know what ur favourite type is, but I know u know mine. We'd have to discuss it. For, um, like, ages. Anyway, really missing u already. But I know I'll see u again. I promise. I'd put everything on the line for it.

We'll be thinking for u.

What advice? Jimmy thought. Georgie hadn't written a single word of advice, and yet that was virtually the only thing his best friend had mentioned.

He read Georgie's part again, over and over, faster and faster, keeping pace with his legs as they powered him up another floor, ever closer to the top of the building. Behind was shouting and the noise of dozens of boots pounding after him. Jimmy shut it out, focusing only on his sister's words. He questioned everything.

A book? What book? Why would she have written to him about books?

"I know you know mine," Jimmy read aloud. Yes, of course he did. One of the sites Jimmy had used last time he had tried to contact Georgie had been an author's website. Suddenly, the rest of the message fell into place. It was as if certain words and phrases shone out, catching the light in a new way.

I'd put everything on *the* line *for it*, Georgie had written. She was telling him to go online. *We'd have to discuss it, For, um, like, ages.* The capital F made it obvious. Georgie was telling him to go to the Forum of the website. And that last line: *We'll be thinking for you.* Jimmy had assumed his sister meant to write "thinking *of* you", but now he realised she was telling him they would come up with a plan for him if he needed them to.

Jimmy broke into a huge smile, even as he strained every muscle to run harder. Now he knew exactly where to go to leave a message for Georgie and Felix. He just had to hope that through them he would be able to get top-secret NJ7 intelligence from Eva about Neptune's Shadow and its connection with Synperco.

He burst through the fire door at the very top of the stairs, on to the roof. The light and cold hit Jimmy with a nasty smack. His breathing was deeper, but still regular. It felt as if his lungs were being held in a fur-lined clamp and gently squeezed to control each breath.

The landscape of the roof was a clutter of concrete blocks, doorways, metal vents, pipes and mobile-phone masts. There was also a huge lightning conductor and an iron tower painted red and white, with an aircraft warning light flashing on the top. The wind gusted in every direction, swirling round Jimmy as he ran. He felt like the centre of a tornado.

He sprinted all the way across the roof, right up to the very edge. In front of him was a huge scaffold structure. It was the back of the Synperco logo that he'd seen from the street. Jimmy didn't hesitate. He peeked over the edge to check the position of the metal struts that attached the logo to the outside of the building. Each one was about half a metre across. It was only a drop of a couple of metres from the roof, but far below that the Manhattan street loomed up to meet Jimmy's eyes. If he missed, he'd be finished.

He carefully lowered himself down, holding on to the laptop with difficulty. Then he dropped the rest of the way. For a split-second, his heart seemed to crunch into a tiny ball. But then his feet landed squarely, right in the centre of one of the struts. Jimmy took a moment to balance himself, then sat down. Just in time – that instant, the roar of the wind was cut by the thrashing blades of a helicopter. Jimmy pressed himself back against the building. He was nestled between the wall and the huge Synperco sign. For now, he couldn't be seen.

While Jimmy powered up the laptop, the chopper circled overhead. Jimmy could just make out the shouts of the security team scouring every centimetre of the roof only a couple of metres above him. As far as they could tell, the only possible explanation was that he had jumped off the building.

Jimmy used the wireless Internet connection to go straight to the right forum. He signed in with the username JawG – just as he had done before. Georgie was sure to recognise it. He didn't have time to think very carefully about his message. He hammered at the keyboard, mouthing the words as he typed:

"Neptune's Shadow – oil base with secret missiles. (till I blew it up.) Now I'm stuck. Ask ur friend what it has 2 do with Synperco and confirm id of man called bligh. Is URGENT. Post reply v v quick or I won't get it."

Then he paused. His fingers hovered over the keys. Finally, he added,

"Thanx. Miss u. Tell F hi."

He tapped the return button, watched his message go up on the message board and slumped back against the cold steel of the building, trying to work out what time of day it was in England. His best chance now was to wait. He had to stay here as long as he possibly could and hope for a response. If the security forces really did believe he'd jumped off the building, their search would move on before long.

But then Jimmy looked around and realised that whether he was found or not, he had no idea how he was going to get back down to the ground.

* * *

Ian Coates stormed out of the Cabinet Room, his aides struggling to keep up. He wound his way through 10 Downing Street, heading straight for the door to the NJ7 bunkers. He had already used this door more than any Prime Minister before him – even Ares Hollingdale. At the threshold, his aides held back, letting him go on alone.

"Miss Bennett!" he roared as soon as he was through into the stark grey corridors. His voice bounced off the concrete. In seconds he had reached her office.

A huge Union Jack flag covered the wall behind the desk, but in the centre of the red, white and blue pattern was a strong green stripe. Miss Bennett was standing between the flag and her desk, her brown curls almost the only soft thing in the whole room. Perched on a stool by the entrance was Eva, in a smaller version of the same black business suit. She had tried to train her hair to tumble about her shoulders like Miss Bennett's, but it hadn't quite worked.

"Miss Bennett!" Coates yelled again. He looked from Miss Bennett to Eva, almost nervously, and tried to keep his authority by lifting his chin and sticking out his chest.

"Are you under the impression that I'm deaf?" Miss Bennett asked, very quietly.

Ian Coates bristled. "You should expend less energy coming up with smart comments and more defending the interests of our country." Miss Bennett tried to interrupt, but the Prime Minister blasted on. "I told you that protecting Neptune's Shadow was a top priority."

"We tried," Miss Bennett replied curtly. "We failed."

"Not good enough," Ian Coates growled, stepping right up to Miss Bennett's desk. There was a metre of leather and wood between them, but to Eva they looked like two wild animals, each one capable of devouring the other at any moment.

"I've just been in a briefing with the Chancellor of the Exchequer," Coates went on, seething, "and he brought me a report from the Department of Trade and Industry."

Miss Bennett raised an eyebrow, inviting Coates to continue.

"It's even worse than I thought. The Neptune's Shadow oil rig was responsible for billions of pounds of annual revenue, not to mention forty per cent of domestic energy. With one blast, France has sabotaged our entire economy. Suddenly, we have no money coming in and the population of Britain might not be able to heat their homes."

"Good job the weather's picked up then," Miss Bennett replied, her expression still ice-cool. She leaned forward on her desk, pushing her face closer to the Prime Minister's, their eyes never parting.

"How can you stand there and pretend you don't care?" asked Coates. "Or that you're not in some way responsible for this failure?"

"Of course I care," Miss Bennett protested. "I care about the money this country has lost, and I care about the man we lost too. Paduk was a hero. He died trying to protect Britain and I'll be recommending him for a posthumous honour. But if we're going to yell at each other every time we suffer a setback – yes, even a major setback like this – how can we ever hope to run this country efficiently? Eva and I were just—"

"You don't run the country, Miss Bennett," the Prime Minister cut in. "I run the country. You run NJ7."

"Yes, Prime Minister," Miss Bennett conceded. Was she slightly overwhelmed by the force in the Prime Minister's voice, Eva wondered, or was she pretending to be? It was difficult to tell.

"Now, show me you can still do your job," Coates ordered. "The French haven't just weakened the country, they've weakened the position of this government. Without that oil, our economy is in trouble. People will start questioning whether we're the right people to have in charge. They'll question the whole Neo-democratic system."

"Thanks for the lesson in politics, Prime Minister, but—"

"Draw up plans to strike France in retaliation," Coates insisted, a rasp in his throat. "Something secret and quick, but devastating."

Eva shrank into the corner, wishing she could

disappear. She had never seen such an intense and unpleasant conversation, with the lives of so many people at stake.

"And the consequences?" Miss Bennett asked, her face only now starting to waver. "It might mean war."

"The consequences," said Coates, "will be that British people will know France is the enemy, not me. A little war now will make sure Britain is run efficiently for a long time to come."

The Prime Minister paused for a moment, watching for Miss Bennett's reaction, but her face didn't reveal what she was thinking. Then he marched out, without glancing in Eva's direction.

31 MR PIGGY GOES TO SCHOOL

Georgie rested her head in her hands, her elbows on her desk. This way she could pretend to be reading her textbook, but actually have her eyes in her lap where her mobile was hidden. Every few seconds it vibrated and another text came in.

Georgie had developed the ability to scan through new text messages very quickly, hardly paying attention to what they said. They weren't from friends. These were automated alerts that arrived every time anybody posted a new message on a particular Internet chatroom.

It was the last lesson of the day and this was the time when her phone was busiest. Georgie's eyes were constantly tired from skimming through text messages, but she couldn't miss a single one in case it was from her brother. She knew that there was every chance Jimmy hadn't even received the birthday note from her and Felix. Even if he had, would he understand what it was telling him to do? *Of course he will*, thought Georgie.

"Georgina Coates!" barked her teacher, a young, overweight man with a straggly black beard. "Are you with us?"

Georgie looked up, deliberately slowly. She was used to this. "Me?" she asked innocently. "Sorry, I was just, like, so interested in the textbook I didn't hear you properly."

Her classmates burst out laughing. Georgie struggled to control her smile while the teacher glared at her. They both knew that she would have trouble even saying what the title of the textbook was – Citizenship lessons had become more and more boring since the Government had brought in the new curriculum.

Georgie didn't wait for her teacher to respond. She had won that small battle. Her phone vibrated again and she casually dropped her head to read the new message, while she flicked through a couple of pages in the textbook. But as soon as she saw the words on the screen of the phone, she gasped. A message from JawG.

She hurriedly read it through.

"That's it, Georgie!" announced her teacher. "You're staying behind."

Georgie looked up, shocked. "But..." she protested.

"Enough!" the teacher shouted. "The atrocities

committed in the name of democracy are not things you should pretend to gasp at."

Georgie was shaking slightly. She couldn't speak. The one moment when her brother needed her and she'd let her guard down.

"I can't stay behind, sir," she said meekly, desperately trying to think of some excuse.

"What do you mean, you can't stay behind?" The teacher's face was glowing red. It made him look a bit like a sunburnt pig. Georgie decided to call him Mr Piggy from now on, at least in her head.

"It's my... my aunt," she stuttered. "She's ill and she's expecting me after school."

"Then I'll get someone in the office to phone her and leave a message that you'll be late." He turned back to the whiteboard.

"No!" Georgie insisted. Her teacher spun round and stared. Georgie's voice came out louder than she'd expected. "She doesn't have a phone."

"She doesn't have a phone?" the teacher squealed. "What sort of person doesn't have a phone?"

"A deaf person," Georgie said immediately. "But my friend Felix... he knows her. He can take her a message. Just let me see him for a second."

There was a long pause. Georgie's teacher furrowed his brow and examined her closely.

"Let me pass on a message to Felix," said Georgie softly,

"and then you can keep me behind as long as you like."

"No." Mr Piggy turned his back and carried on writing up a list of dates on the whiteboard.

Jimmy said he needed a response urgently. What kind of danger was he in? Georgie's imagination took her by surprise with the terror it planted in her mind. If she didn't act until she was out of school, it might be too late.

She quickly memorised Jimmy's message, then pummelled her phone's keypad with her thumbs. Whenever Mr Piggy looked up at the class she paused for a second, her heart pounding. At last she hit 'send' and Jimmy's message was passed on, word for word, to Eva.

For the rest of the lesson Georgie couldn't sit still. Tension wrenched every muscle. The sounds of the classroom faded into the background. All she could do was wait.

Mr Piggy only kept Georgie after school for about ten minutes, but to her it seemed like hours. When she finally ran out of the gate, Felix was waiting for her.

"What happened?" he asked.

"Long story," said Georgie. "But look." She showed Felix the message from Jimmy.

"That must be from him!" Felix shouted, bouncing along the street. "He blew up some secret missiles! That is so cool."

"Hey!" Georgie snapped. "You want to say that a bit louder?"

"Sorry." Felix grabbed the phone again and re-read Jimmy's message. "What's Synperco?" he whispered.

Georgie shrugged.

"Did you pass this on to Auntie?" Felix asked.

"Of course, now will you shut up about it?"

Felix nodded frantically and pulled an imaginary zip across his lips.

"Oh," Georgie went on, "if anybody at school asks you, my aunt is deaf."

"What?" Felix gasped under his breath. He leaned in closer to Georgie as they walked. "Eva's gone deaf?"

"No, you idiot. But just say that my aunt has if anyone asks."

Felix paused for a second of thought, then asked, "You actually have an aunt?"

"Well, yeah," Georgie sighed. "I actually do. They're not an endangered species. But she's not deaf. Anyway, you know what I mean."

There was a long silence. Then, just as they reached the bus stop, Felix couldn't contain his confusion any more.

"So wait," he blurted out. "Is she, or isn't she, you know, deaf?"

Georgie punched him on the shoulder.

* * *

Eva was aware of Miss Bennett staring in her direction, but she had to trust that her boss had no reason to watch her. Eva carried on transferring information from her main NJ7 computer to her palmtop. *Calm*, she told herself. *Natural. This is normal.* And yet at the same time, her heart was thumping. If Miss Bennett happened to see what Eva was really doing, she was finished.

Miss Bennett sighed. "I'm glad I trusted my instincts about you, Eva," she announced. "And I have a report here that says your brothers' training is going very well."

Eva took a second before replying. She measured every breath she took. "Good," she murmured, not looking away from her computer. "I mean, that's great."

"But sometimes," Miss Bennett went on, "even the best get found out."

Eva's entire body tensed up. *She knows*, she thought. *Oh God, she knows.* Still she held her poise and carried on working at the computer. Whatever happened, she had to get this message back to Georgie.

"And I want you to know," said Miss Bennett wistfully, "that your brothers might eventually have to enter a combat situation. And that if anything happens to them..."

Eva could feel her muscles petrifying. Was Miss Bennett threatening her?

"Well, Eva," Miss Bennett continued. "Let's just say they'll be heroes."

Eva's breathing stopped. At last she turned. Miss Bennett was standing over her desk, rotating two shiny stones in her hand, one black, one white. There were more like them on the desk, arranged on a checked board.

"Heroes?" Eva whimpered.

Miss Bennett nodded slowly and dropped her eyes to the stones on the board. There was a moment's silence. Eva's fear was dampened by her confusion. Then suddenly, Miss Bennett looked up, her eyes wide, and asked in a bright tone, "Do you know how to play this game?"

Eva's shock and relief made her voice squeak. "No," she replied. "No, I'm afraid I don't."

By the time Felix and Georgie had received a reply from Eva, and posted that reply on the Internet, Jimmy had been hidden at the top of the Synperco building for nearly two hours. Despite the shelter of the giant logo, the wind was still blasting into him. He'd tried everything he could think of to crack the encryption of Bligh's files, but without any luck, and every minute or two he was checking for new messages on the website.

When the reply finally came, Jimmy could hardly believe that their method of communication had worked. Before he even read what it said, he felt a surge of emotion. The message was from someone called GJaw. That alone told Jimmy that somewhere on the other side of the Atlantic, his sister and his best friend were still thinking of him. Even though they were thousands of miles apart, and any communication between them risked all their lives, Jimmy felt as close to them now as he ever had.

He leaned forward, closer to the screen, ignoring the 300-metre drop to the ground. The wind was blowing grit into his eyes. Then he noticed that the battery on the laptop was running down. He read the message quickly.

"Don't understand. What secret missiles? N.S. just a big oil rig. No connection with Synperco except it's an oil company. Everyone thinks Zafi blew up N.S. so UK planning attack on France. Who's Bligh? Not one of ours."

What secret missiles? The question swirled round Jimmy's head. He pictured the huge storage tanks he'd found on the rig and flinched at the memory of the oil surrounding him, pulling him under. Surely the missiles had been hidden somewhere else on the base? Jimmy felt confusion washing through him. Eva had to be wrong. Why would the CIA think

Neptune's Shadow was a secret missile base if there was nothing there but oil? With such sophisticated surveillance hardware, how could they have got it wrong?

Then another line of the message hit him. *UK planning attack on France.*

Of course, Jimmy thought. Only Paduk had realised that the assassin destroying Neptune's Shadow was Jimmy, not Zafi.

Jimmy's lungs clenched in horror, making it hard for him to breathe. *What have I done?* he asked himself. *Instead of stopping a war, I might have accidentally started one.*

Then he focused on the last line: *Who's Bligh? Not one of ours.* Jimmy read it over and over. He couldn't take his eyes off the word "ours". Was Eva becoming one of them? He told himself she must have written her answer in a hurry and, what's more, probably didn't want to type NJ7 in case the message was flagged up by an automatic scan. Jimmy had acted with the same caution. But to use the word "ours", as if Eva really belonged to that organisation of murderers and thieves… Jimmy shuddered.

He put his hands over the keys, ready to bash out a reply. But in the corner of his eye he caught sight of a black ball creeping through the sky towards him. He looked up. It was another helicopter. Jimmy's programming kicked him from the inside.

Instead of moving the search to the ground or calling it off completely, Synperco security had called in more high-tech equipment. Jimmy knew instantly that there would be heat sensors on that second chopper. His hiding place was useless. But Jimmy hadn't just been sitting there all this time, waiting for a message. He'd been working out exactly how he could get to the ground without being caught. And this was the perfect moment to put his plan into action.

32 ABSEILING ONLINE

Jimmy rubbed his hands together to warm his fingers a little. Then he shut down the laptop and dismantled it, piece by piece. First he removed the battery pack, the hard disk and the CD-ROM drive. Then he dug his nail in at the edge of the keyboard and pulled it open to reveal the rest of the inner workings of the computer. It was still hot, but Jimmy didn't mind that. It would only help the circulation to his fingers.

Calmly and methodically, he disconnected all the separate components from the system board and lined them up carefully on the metal strut in front of him. Alongside the small fan, the CPU card, the disk controller and the rest, was the most important part of all: almost a metre of cable. Jimmy unravelled it and tested its strength with a tug. Would it take his weight? He had no idea, but didn't have a choice.

He threaded the cable through the empty casing of

the laptop and wrapped it round his waist. It was barely long enough to go all the way round. Jimmy sucked his stomach in. The black plastic of the laptop casing went behind him to protect the small of his back, then he took the two ends of the cable and tied them in front of him, through the fan holes in the disk controller.

The cable dug into his sides, but this wasn't meant to feel good. It was meant to get him to the ground in a way that didn't end with a splat. And the tiny part of the laptop that was going to make that possible was the silver metal hook sticking out of the disk controller – part of the eject mechanism.

With his makeshift belt in place, Jimmy crouched, waiting for the helicopters to circle round the other side of the building. Then he stretched up and jumped to catch the rim of the roof. The wind roared around him, as if it was going to lift him into the sky, then throw him down to destruction. He could feel the strain starting in the tips of his fingers, running down his arms and all the way down his spine. But his muscles were locked in position. Brushing his nose was the cold black glass of the building, showing him a gruesome, too-close reflection of the exertion on his own face. Only one thought kept running through his mind: *Don't look down.*

He moved quickly, but carefully, an arm's length at a time. In less than a minute he'd made it to the corner of the building. That's when the helicopters came zooming round into view. They didn't need their heat sensors now – Jimmy was dangling off the building in plain sight. It didn't matter. He had made it as far round as he needed to. At this corner of the skyscraper a thin strip of metal ran all the way to the ground – the lightning conductor.

Still holding on to the roof with both hands, Jimmy manoeuvred his body until the eject mechanism on his improvised belt hooked round the lightning conductor. Then, without even hesitating, he let go of the building.

He fell at an incredible pace. The corner of the skyscraper rushed past his face, making his drop seem even faster. He had no time to waste. He was in freefall and unless he wrestled back control he would be a puddle on the New York sidewalk before he had time to take a breath.

He stuck his legs out, scraping the backs of his heels against the sides of the building. His whole body throbbed with the vibrations and his feet burned. In the wind, his eyes were watering so much he could hardly see. His mind was constantly battling panic.

He pushed all his strength into his legs, keeping good contact and increasing the friction. Then he leaned back, as far as he could. The laptop cable stretched with the pressure, but it held. Every few metres was another bolt where the lightning conductor was attached to the building. Each time

Jimmy passed one, his hook jumped off. He gripped the cable with one hand, and with the other, forced the hook back on to the metal rod every time.

Now his pace was slowing. Within five seconds he was used to the rhythm of the bolts passing him and he could prepare for them, pulling his hook off and immediately slamming it back on again. The cable round his waist kept stretching, until Jimmy was leaning all the way back with his legs horizontal, but bent at the knee. It was the perfect position in which to control the pace of his fall. He knew the landing would still be painful, but it wouldn't be fatal.

In no time, the force of the wind dropped and Jimmy became aware of the noise of Manhattan traffic. He braced himself for impact. His hook was glowing orange from the heat of the friction. One more second and it snapped off.

With nothing to hold him to the building, Jimmy fell backwards. He tumbled head over heels through the air with no idea how much distance there was between him and the ground. But he'd done enough.

He smacked into the pavement less than a second after coming free from the lightning conductor. He landed square on his back. The impact blasted all the air out of his lungs. For a few seconds he stayed like that, staring up at the sky, unable to breathe. Two black dots circled over him. Everybody had seen him fall. Now he could feel them watching to see whether he was alive.

Then, at last, his shock melted into delight. He couldn't believe that a length of laptop cable and a lightning conductor had enabled him to slide all the way down the corner of a seventy-storey skyscraper. His breathing eased to a more natural rate. His cheeks were flushed and there was a huge smile on his face.

That vanished as soon as he saw one of the helicopters floating down, carefully balancing over the junction. To a blaring symphony of horns, a squad of US Marines dropped down a rope ladder, flooding the street. They charged towards Jimmy.

Jimmy rolled over and propped himself up on his elbow. He didn't know whether to run. His programming buzzed inside him, but didn't compel him to move. It was Synperco security he'd had to avoid. Had the CIA told the Marines about him? If so, they were on his side. If not, they would either arrest him, try to kill him or at least want to know who he was. Any of those options would be a disaster.

"It's OK, Jimmy," came a man's voice behind him. Jimmy jumped up into a combat stance, ready for trouble. There, leaning against the Synperco building, was the CIA agent who had tried to escort him from Brooklyn – the grey-haired man with trout lips. He was still chewing his gum.

"These guys are here to secure the building for

Synperco," he said, lips smacking. He had read the indecision on Jimmy's face. "Nobody knows about you. They were worried about a terrorist attack. Everyone might be evacuating in a minute."

Jimmy turned back to the helicopter. It was still hovering there, blowing up all of the dust and trash from the street while the soldiers took up their positions around the block. But Jimmy didn't relax. Could he trust this man? He seemed to have Jimmy's interests in mind now, but what about earlier, when he'd refused to believe that Bligh was still alive? Jimmy felt the urgency of making the right call. The security of CIA secrets depended on it.

"Listen," he started, trying not to sound crazy, and watching all the time for the man's reaction. "Agent Bligh. He was in there." He nodded towards the building. "I know you don't believe me, but he's still alive and he's working for Synperco. I think he's a double agent. For some reason he needed the rest of the CIA to think that he'd been killed, but he wasn't."

The trout-faced agent walked silently towards Jimmy, no emotion on his face. "Got evidence?" he grunted.

"I got his laptop," Jimmy began, looking down at his shoes. "But I had to take it apart." Then he looked up suddenly and shouted, "What evidence do you need, anyway? Call Keays now! Go in there and you'll find Bligh on the fifty-seventh floor. He's probably still throwing up in the toilets."

The agent nodded slowly and scratched his ear, as if he was considering Jimmy's words. He was standing very close now, so Jimmy had to look up to see his face. The man was surveying the chaos in the street, his square jaw rocking from side to side as he chewed.

"Probably," he muttered.

"What's the matter with you?" Jimmy yelled, holding his hands out in exasperation, horror rising in his chest. "Bligh is alive! Are you going to call Keays?" He spoke slowly, sounding out every word. "Bligh's working for Synperco."

"Jimmy," replied the agent, suddenly fixing him with a stare, "we all work for Synperco."

His voice was soft, but Jimmy heard perfectly. The words seeped into Jimmy's head and then seemed to explode. His whole head rocked from the inside. His worst fears had been confirmed.

"I knew it," he gasped. "Double agents." He staggered backwards, as if the agent in front of him was exuding some foul smell. "Synperco used the CIA to destroy a rival oil rig? Is that it?" Jimmy was whispering, working it out as he spoke. "A team of double agents..." In a flash he pieced it together – the false information about Neptune's Shadow coming from Bligh, and Jimmy faithfully taking it to Colonel Keays, so that Keays would send him to destroy the rig.

"You..." Jimmy stared straight ahead. His anger and shock were so powerful they seemed to steal the words from his mouth, but he forced himself to speak. "They used the CIA!" he shouted. "Then they used me. *You* used me!" He stared up at the trout-faced agent, who was still anxiously looking around to see who might be watching them. But the helicopter was enough of a distraction for everybody else in the street.

"Keep your voice down," said the agent casually, still not looking at Jimmy. "Nobody else needs to know."

"But... But..." Jimmy kept backing away. The agent stepped slowly after him.

"Quiet, Jimmy. Everything's going to be fine. Come with me and you'll be safe. There's a CIA safehouse waiting."

"A *safehouse*?" Jimmy spat out the word in disgust. "How can you say that when you work... for them." He stretched out his arm towards the building's entrance and pointed at the huge grey S beneath the flagpole.

"It's complicated," the man replied. "You won't understand. Now, just keep your voice down."

"*Keep my voice down?*" Jimmy yelled as hard as he could. "About Synperco and the—"

"Be quiet, Jimmy."

It wasn't the words that cut Jimmy off. It was the Beretta pistol the agent pulled from under his jacket. He held it at hip height, the barrel directed at Jimmy's throat. Then he repeated, in a slow whisper, "I said, be quiet, Jimmy."

33 FLYING A FLAG

The sight of the gun struck something deep inside Jimmy. It felt like he was seeing it not just with his eyes, but with his gut. His body's reaction was immediate and violent. He threw himself into a forward roll. As his legs arched over his body, Jimmy flicked his left foot. His heel hammered into the agent's right wrist. The scaphoid bone shattered with the sound of a Christmas cracker and the gun dropped to the ground.

Jimmy dashed to the Synperco building. He used the doors to clamber up the frontage and pulled himself up on the grey S of the company logo. He could feel his temples throbbing with the surge of adrenaline. Every move he made surprised him a little more. His programming had never felt so strong. At some point, without Jimmy even being aware of the change, it had developed a determination of its own.

He grabbed the flagpole with both hands and dangled from it, as the CIA agent struggled to command the security forces around the building. The noise of the helicopter and the chaos of the general public worked in Jimmy's favour. He knew that with so many forces on the scene there was only one means of transport available to him that was fast enough to make his escape. It was hovering in the middle of the junction.

With the American flag fluttering against his body, Jimmy calmly untied the knots of the rope that held it up. Meanwhile, the loop of laptop cable was still round his waist. It was slipping down to his knees now, but Jimmy didn't mind. He kicked it off, then let go of the flagpole.

He caught the laptop cable in mid-air as he fell, then ran to the centre of the junction, dodging the traffic and dragging the flag rope behind him. Debris blasted into him, thrown up by the mini-tornado from the helicopter's rotor. As he ran he fastened one end of the flag rope to the loop of cable. The helicopter was steadily rising – a technical challenge in such a built-up space. The rope ladder was gone, but Jimmy didn't need it.

He swirled the loop of cable over his head like a cowboy's lasso. The chopper was rising more quickly every second, now that the pilot had noticed what Jimmy was about to attempt.

Jimmy jumped on to the roof of a yellow cab and

immediately pushed himself off again, hurling his lasso into the sky. His leap was totally efficient: muscles relaxed, limbs still. His throw was perfect. The loop of cable hooked just over the front end of the helicopter's runner.

At the peak of his jump he clasped the rope. It pulled taut with a nasty jerk. The American flag fluttered proudly further down the rope, upside-down. Immediately, Jimmy hauled himself up, fist over fist. The helicopter was surging upwards now, easily compensating for the lopsided weight hanging from one runner. It leaned to the side for only a second before levelling out and pulling higher.

In Jimmy's ears, the shouting below was drowned out by the chopper's rotor. His biceps trembled with the power surging through them. In no time, Jimmy could hook his elbows over the runner and reach up for the tread that ran round the body of the helicopter.

Nobody could stop him. Even if the pilot had known exactly where Jimmy was, there was nothing he could have done. The chopper was trapped a quarter of the way up the skyscrapers. He couldn't shake Jimmy off by banking sharply to one side, and he couldn't land – the street below was only now coming under the control of the armed forces and being cleared.

With one heave, Jimmy flipped through the open side of the helicopter and rolled across the floor.

He jumped to his feet and charged to the front of the cockpit. The pilot was a lightly built man in combat armour and a black helmet. He was also quick.

In one movement, the pilot twisted away from his controls and dipped his hand to his hip. It came up flashing a gun, but Jimmy was there already. He dropped to his knees, spun full circle on the metal and crashed his elbow into the pilot's grip. He followed with a jab to the man's Adam's apple, temporarily cutting off the air to his lungs.

The pilot was powerless now. Jimmy heaved him out of the flight seat and tumbled him over the edge of the chopper. The man bounced on to the roof of the taxi that Jimmy had jumped off. He shook off help from his fellow Marines and yelled at the skies in frustration.

Jimmy wasn't even watching. He was already sitting at the flight controls. *I've done this before*, he told himself with a deep breath. *I can do it again.* And yet at the same time, he could feel the strange but absolute assurance within him that this helicopter was totally different to the one he'd flown along the Thames all that time ago.

UH-2Z Huey. The make and model throbbed in his skull as his eyes took in the display. There were two twenty-centimetre square LCD screens in front of him, and another that was about half the size. In the centre of it all was a data entry console. There was no joystick.

Then Jimmy looked up. Through the window of an office building he locked eyes with a stunned secretary. They were barely metres from each other. Jimmy smiled and winked. The secretary screamed – not that Jimmy heard, of course. All he could hear was the drone of the chopper and a calming voice in his head that sounded like the beat of a military band: *Steady, steady, steady.*

Even as the soldiers below opened fire, Jimmy trusted what his instincts were telling him, despite his senses screaming danger. He knew that the Integrated Avionics and Stability Control Augmentation System would keep the Huey steady without any human interference. All Jimmy had to do was tell it to lift him straight up, avoiding the skyscrapers, and set a directional heading once he was clear of the buildings.

Jimmy tapped the screen in a couple of places, so quickly that he didn't even catch what the display said before it changed. The chopper responded with a growl and continued its rise towards the clouds. *It almost has a mind of its own*, Jimmy thought. Then came a sinister echo in his head that added, *Like me.*

He shuddered and distracted himself by leaning forwards to peer out of the front of the helicopter. The street was lurching away from him. The chopper picked up pace. Jimmy surged past Synperco's giant S and was suddenly overlooking the roofs of the skyscrapers.

Jimmy could feel something turning over inside him as fast as the twin 2000-horsepower engines of the Huey. His eyes were no longer in his control. He wanted to look around at his position in the sky and take a second to work out what he was going to do. But his programming had all the information it needed from the Northrop Grumman radar warning receiver. His console flashed with a million tiny pieces of information, all of them vital, and all of them instantly absorbed and processed by the operating system that was Jimmy's brain.

They're coming, he told himself. Fighter jets. They'd been scrambled to take him out of the Manhattan skies, and they would be there within seconds.

Jimmy was so desperate to keep control of his thoughts that he grunted aloud, "Double agents." His voice croaked, battling the rest of his body to be heard. "Colonel Keays has to know."

His own words were drowned out by the thundering truth in his head. He had no idea where Keays was. *Forget Keays. Destroy Synperco.* It was the perfect assassin inside him, driving his body to act with complete efficiency. With the double agents working against him, there was no way Jimmy would be able to reach Colonel Keays, even if he did know where the man was. Didn't it make more sense to deal with the problem by himself?

Destroy Synperco. It came again. He felt it more than he heard it. There was no voice whispering these things to him, just a wave of overpowering realisation.

"No!" Jimmy shouted, but he almost choked on the word and coughed violently.

His body convulsed with the conflict inside him. He had never felt his programming tearing at him quite like this, as if it wanted to spit out his soul and carry on without it.

Jimmy had to close his eyes. His face scrunched into a hideous grimace. He could feel his human protest crumbling. He couldn't get it to make sense. A tear escaped and raced down his cheek.

But then, suddenly, his muscles relaxed. There was another way to bring down Synperco and its network of double agents. He could even get the names of the agents. All he needed was five minutes with the director of the company. And from somewhere within Jimmy's psyche came the information he needed.

It had been the first thing he'd seen on Bligh's laptop – some kind of flight plan involving the company director. Jimmy didn't know whether it was his programming or his human memory that had retained the information. For now it didn't matter.

But all he had were the words "Director", "Flight" and a string of numbers. Even if he could remember the numbers, what did they mean? Would they tell him for sure that the director was flying somewhere? If so, where from? And when?

Jimmy closed his eyes. He tried to picture the document exactly the way it had appeared. He could see the bold black letters saying "Director", but nothing else. Just then the helicopter console emitted a short beep. The fighter jets were closing in.

34 FINDING VIGGO

Georgie and Felix sat staring at a gameshow on the TV. Neither of them was paying any attention to it, nor even to the food that was on their laps – another microwave meal. Felix shovelled it into his mouth automatically.

The sofa irritated him through his trousers and the whole living room smelled strongly of air freshener. Felix secretly quite liked the smell, though the itching was annoying.

"Would you stop wriggling?" Georgie muttered. "I'm getting chicken korma on my uniform."

Felix wasn't listening. The only thing on his mind was Jimmy's message and the reply they'd passed on from Eva. He pictured his friend in dozens of different locations, always extremely dangerous ones. He started by imagining different parts of New York City, then moved on to other parts of America, but he had never actually seen any of those so they quickly became strange fantasies involving cowboys, pirates and occasionally an alien.

Then he pictured Jimmy in thick jungle, being held at gunpoint by a man in a gorilla costume. Deep down he knew that every scenario was ridiculous. Whenever he tried to work out a realistic picture of what Jimmy was doing, there was only blackness and a feeling of terror. It was much easier to fill in the blanks with daydreams that couldn't possibly be real.

There was a click at the front door. Felix snapped out of his imagination. He was always on alert, although he knew it would just be Jimmy's mum. She was home at around this time every evening.

She walked in and gave them a nod. Nobody said anything. They never did. They knew the whole flat was bugged and probably fitted with cameras too. For the first few days they had staged fake conversations in very loud voices, trying to mislead NJ7, but now they didn't bother.

Instead, Georgie picked up the remote control and turned up the volume on the TV to maximum. Then the three of them sat close together on the sofa, with Helen in the middle. They dropped their heads to their laps so that nobody could read their lips on camera. This had become their routine.

"I think I know where Chris and Saffron have been

hiding," Helen said softly. Georgie and Felix leaned in closer so that they didn't miss a word.

"The restaurant?" Georgie guessed. When Jimmy had first tracked him down, Christopher Viggo had been running his opposition to the Government from a Turkish restaurant.

"It's boarded up," Helen replied, shaking her head. "It wouldn't be safe to go back, but I think he's left most of his belongings there."

"So where?" asked Felix.

"I can't be sure," Helen replied. "I'm going to need a bit more time. I'm watched wherever I go and I have to look like I'm finding a job. But I want you two to know I'm making progress. I've also found out about an organisation that campaigns for all the British people who've disappeared." She glanced at Felix, then immediately looked away. "They're based in France, so I don't know how to get in touch with them yet, but everything's going to be OK. We can campaign legitimately and at the same time find out where NJ7 are keeping your mum and dad, Felix."

Felix sucked on his bottom lip.

"Once I've found Chris we can work together," Helen went on. "If I know him at all, he's in London and he's making plans. He knows we're here, and he'll make contact when it's safe. With a little time, we'll find a way. OK?"

Georgie and Felix nodded.

"Good," said Helen, relaxing her shoulders and leaning back on the sofa. "Now, how was school?"

She took the remote from Georgie and started turning the TV volume back down. Georgie and Felix looked at each other. Felix reached out and gently slipped the remote out of Helen's hand. She looked at him, shocked at first, but then read his serious expression. Felix steadily increased the TV volume again.

At the same time, Georgie pulled her mobile phone from her pocket and held it out so her mother could see the screen while she scrolled through the text messages. The TV got louder and louder. Felix loved the feeling of the noise booming round his head. It felt like having a soapy bath for his brain.

At last they were talking about Jimmy – not Chris, not Saffron and not Eva. Jimmy was the one person Felix knew had been on all their minds most, but that they'd talked about least.

Helen Coates broke down, sobbing, in her daughter's arms.

35 BLACK WIDOWS

Jimmy's eyes flashed open. Three flat black planes were charging towards him from the edge of Manhattan, leaving trails of grey smoke behind them. To Jimmy they were immediately recognisable as Black Widow II Fighter Jets, shaped like stingrays, but with sharper points – and more missiles.

His hands moved with a short, sharp rhythm, never hesitating. He tapped the console three or four times a second, adding layer upon layer to the instructions. The helicopter suddenly banked to the side and dropped at the same time.

Jimmy's only advantage over the planes was the ability to manoeuvre between buildings. He guided the chopper down, beneath the level of the skyscrapers. He dipped between them, picking up speed, rolling the chopper round every corner. He was like a mouse scurrying through long grass to escape three eagles. He changed direction at every opportunity, twisting through the grid of Manhattan. The thrill of the flight sent a smile to Jimmy's face. Then he caught a glimpse of the Black Widows above him. They thundered overhead. Jimmy knew he had a few precious seconds before they made another pass.

Focus, he told himself. He tried to drag up every detail of the document he'd seen on Bligh's computer, right down to the curve of the screen and the reflection of the lights. But Jimmy had only glanced at it and chosen to ignore it completely. Then something in him clicked. A picture of Bligh's document suddenly expanded in his memory.

Under the word "Director" was a string of numbers. The digits jumped from his memory to his lips: "43.01569." He took a breath, unable to believe what he was saying. Then came more. "77.57034." Straightaway, he pounded the console screen with the pads of his index fingers. The numbers were co-ordinates.

The Huey lurched upwards, leaving Jimmy's stomach behind. The engines snarled. He soared above the streets, higher and higher, until the grid became a grey jumble. Then he powered forwards on his new course. According to the console, Jimmy was heading for Rochester on the northern outskirts of New York City.

Jimmy frowned. There was something more

throbbing in his head. The number string wasn't over. The last digits crept up on him: 13:01. That could only be one thing – the time of the flight. Jimmy looked at the top of the small LCD screen. His estimated flight time was fifty-eight minutes. Next to that was the time – 12:28.

"No!" Jimmy shouted. He banged his fist on the console screen. Then he frantically hit more buttons, begging the Huey to move faster and faster. The metal casing of the cockpit started rattling. Jimmy didn't care. He stared at the numbers on his screen. It was 12:30. He'd cut his estimated flight time to forty-one minutes.

Jimmy could hardly hear himself think now for the noise in the cockpit, but still he kept adjusting the chopper's navigation settings, desperate for that extra speed. He had to make it in time. If he missed this chance to confront the Director of Synperco, when would he ever get another one?

His manipulation of the controls was beginning to work. Gradually, his speed increased and his estimated flight time came down. Now the computer was telling him he would run out of fuel if he maintained this velocity. *I'll deal with that when it happens*, thought Jimmy. Then...

BOOM!

Even compared to the din of the helicopter, this noise was immense. For a moment, Jimmy's head swum. The Black Widows were back and they'd broken the sound barrier to catch up with him.

The tall buildings of Manhattan were far behind now. There was nothing to shelter Jimmy. Every second he had to change heading, swooping from high altitude to low and back again. His fingers tapped on the console with the intensity of African drumming. He was turning the speed of the planes into a disadvantage. They couldn't twist and turn to stay alongside Jimmy and control where he flew.

But a signal from them flashed up on one of Jimmy's screens. It was a warning, ordering him to slow down, head to a particular spot and land safely. Jimmy didn't even bother reading it all. But he knew what the next step would be. The army was probably already evacuating a region up ahead so that the planes could shoot him down.

Then he heard the frantic beeping of his warning system. It was happening already. The Huey deployed its countermeasures automatically, starting with a screen of chaff. But Jimmy knew they could only be temporary protection. Then came the first strikes. As expected, the missiles from the fighter jets detonated in the chaff. The explosion rocked the cockpit, but at least the helicopter was still in one piece.

Jimmy used the cover of the violent firework display to dive straight down, until he was low enough to read the number plates on the cars lined up in the suburban driveways. People were hurrying to evacuate, under the guidance of uniformed soldiers.

The UH-2Z Huey pounded onwards. Jimmy never allowed the speed to drop, even now that the fuel warning light was constantly flashing. He glanced at the console to find out his estimated flight time. Instead of a number, there was only a flashing red question mark. Jimmy allowed himself a dry laugh. The computer had become so confused by his flying that it had given up trying to predict his movements.

Jimmy switched his screen to a map view and rose back into the sky. According to the co-ordinates, he was close to his destination. He peered out of the wide glass dome that made up the front of the helicopter. He had to squint against the brightness of the sky. The sun glinted off every rooftop below him. He looked further ahead, searching for anything that looked like an airfield, or even a solitary runway.

Then his breath caught in his throat. Up ahead was a rough patch of land surrounded by a barbed-wire fence that looked huge even from up in the sky. The field was divided by two grey stripes – runways.

As he approached, Jimmy saw more detail. He watched in horror as a small private plane taxied to the end of one runway, then immediately zipped along it and took off. He narrowed his eyes to look closer.

Was that a grey circle on the side of the plane, with a black S stamped on top? It had to be. Jimmy looked at the time. 13:03. The Director's holiday had started two minutes behind schedule.

Jimmy clenched his jaw. The Huey couldn't move any faster. According to the computer, there was no fuel left in the tank. Jimmy was flying on nothing but desperation. The closer he came to the airfield, the further the small grey plane flew away.

Then Jimmy heard the warning system beeping again. For a second, he thought he could hear missiles whizzing towards him. He couldn't breathe. His muscles braced for the impact. His mind felt like it had frozen, waiting for death. But somewhere underneath the fear, there was something that wouldn't let go. It was like a tiny ball of flame inside an ice brick. The more the cold and pressure built up around it, the more intensely it burned.

As soon as Jimmy felt that flame, he willed it to take over. And with that will came power. He had seconds to save himself. The engines of the helicopter were spluttering. The rotor was failing. But for now, the computer was still working.

Jimmy leaned back in his seat and kicked out with both his heels at the cockpit glass. It felt as hard as steel, but with three pinpointed kicks, Jimmy smashed it. The wind attacked his face. Fragments of glass peppered his skin. He brushed them off, cleared the console and tapped on one of the screens. A flap at his elbow clicked open and a trigger appeared. Without a fraction of hesitation, he lifted his hand to the trigger and squeezed.

He felt a rumble in the floor of the cockpit. At the same time he heard the high-pitched squeal of the Black Widow missiles tearing towards the back of the Huey. Jimmy crouched on his seat and leaned forwards.

THUD!

The missiles hit, ripping through the back rotor of the helicopter. The whole chopper jerked forwards with the impact. Jimmy was thrown forwards, straight out of the hole he'd created in the glass. He stretched his arms above his head in a dive.

BOOM!

The Huey disintegrated in a ball of flame – but not before a single missile fizzed out from underneath. Jimmy had engaged the firing mechanism just before the Huey was hit. The explosion hurtled Jimmy forwards. The heat on his back felt like the jaws of a tiger mauling him. This was the split-second that counted.

In the flames and the smoke, Jimmy couldn't see anything. But he was listening. Alongside the BOOM was the fizz of the Huey's missile. He reached out blindly, groping in the direction of the noise. His fingers grasped the burning hot metal. *Got it!* The pain was fierce, but letting go would mean plummeting to his death. The missile was Jimmy's express ticket to safety.

The flaming ball of the helicopter crashed downwards. Ahead of it, Jimmy streaked through the sky, hanging beneath the slim body of the Huey's 70mm Mk86 rocket.

36 PROMISES BROKEN

Jimmy was dragged through the sky like a rat trapped in the claws of an eagle. He clung on, a hand either side of the rocket, hanging from it with his arms above his head. He couldn't have let go even if he'd wanted to. The heat of the rocket had grafted his hands to the metal. The scorching sensation seemed to rip down the length of his arms, stabbing at his nerves.

He crunched his muscles to swing his legs forwards, fighting the G-force and the wind thrashing into him. On the fourth attempt he threw his ankles round the tip of the rocket. Then he ripped his right hand off the metal in a single, sudden motion.

He howled in agony, but his scream was lost in the sky. There were only patches of skin left on his palm. The rest was spitting blood in the wind, so thick with the stuff it looked almost black, and beneath the blood was a strange layer of dull grey.

The rocket's squeal was rising in pitch as it approached the target. The explosive was charging. The target was the one Jimmy had programmed in before diving from the helicopter – the small Synperco plane that he'd just watched taking off.

Jimmy used his bloodied right hand to pick open a panel on the rocket. Beneath the panel was a circuit board. Jimmy ripped it out with one huge drag. The high-pitched squeal stopped immediately, leaving only the roar of the wind.

But along with the electronic charge for the explosives, Jimmy had torn out the missile's guidance system. What had been a direct flight to his destination was now a runaway rocket. Jimmy had to take control. He twisted his knees this way and that, trying to work out what effect it had. Too late. The plane was too close.

THUMP!

Jimmy's back slammed into the side of the plane, above the wing. He felt each rib clattering. He thought his lungs were going to burst. The rocket charged on, tearing the skin from Jimmy's left hand. Pain seared through his whole body, but he'd done enough to divert the rocket's course. It roared on through the sky, falling safely to earth in a steady arc.

Jimmy tumbled over himself and landed on his head on the plane's wing. The Falcon 20 was a small jet, only about sixteen metres from tip to tail, but it was one of the fastest light aircraft on the market. So soon after take-off it had already reached nearly 500 miles an hour.

Jimmy came to his senses just in time to plant his hands on the wing, holding himself on. His arms throbbed as he gripped, the incredible pain from his palms hardly relenting. He felt like his eyes were going to be blown from their sockets if he opened them too wide. He turned his head for some shelter and crawled forwards on the wing. It was marked with the Synperco logo, but now the black 'S' was smeared with Jimmy's blood.

He peeked over the edge of the wing. The ground hurtled by. After a second, the sight made Jimmy's stomach churn, so he let the world fall out of focus into a whirl of greys, greens and browns.

His bones vibrated with the plane. He clenched his jaw to stop his teeth hammering together. Then he let go of the wing with his left hand, and the strain on his right arm doubled. He scrabbled at the body of the plane, leaving dark red trails on the polished white.

At last he clutched the emergency release of the cabin door in his fingertips. He tensed his arm and the cabin door flew open. Jimmy crawled towards the opening and tumbled into the plane. He had just made it. If the plane had climbed any higher, the air pressurisation inside would have forced everything out as soon as the door was open a crack.

Jimmy fell with no control, thudding on to thick blue

carpet, face down. He heard two men shouting to each other.

"What the...?" yelled a deep, male voice, with an American twang. "Quick! Tell the pilot!"

"He'll know, sir," replied another American voice. "He has a warning system. Look – our speed has dropped already."

Then Jimmy heard the banging of the cabin door being heaved back into place.

"Is it safe to carry on up here?" shouted the first voice. "Do we need to land?"

"I'll check with the pilot, sir."

Jimmy pushed himself on to all fours, making dark handprints on the carpet. The plane jolted from side to side. It was taking a few seconds for the pilot to steady the flight after the disruption of the cabin being breached. Meanwhile, Jimmy could feel murder in his muscles. *I'll kill them all*, he heard himself thinking. *Everybody on the plane.*

Jimmy breathed deeply, desperate to calm himself. He had to tame it – that assassin's instinct, driving him to kill. *But that's what they deserve*, he thought. *They made me cause a war.* Jimmy squeezed his eyes closed and shut out the rest of the world.

I shouldn't have come, a tiny voice in his head protested. But then Jimmy pushed himself to his feet, drew his shoulders back and held his head up. *Keep control*, he ordered himself over and over again. *Get the names of the double agents and take them back to Colonel Keays.*

At last Jimmy was ready. The plane was perfectly steady again, and Jimmy felt soothed by the hum of the white noise. The cabin of the plane was only about two metres wide and Jimmy planted his feet firmly in the centre, facing the back of the plane. Then he opened his eyes.

In front of him was a stocky, middle-aged man, with thinning brown hair and sagging cheeks that wobbled with the vibrations of the flight. He was leaning back in the centre of a double seat of white leather that ran across the width of the plane. His arms were stretched out along the back of the seat on either side of him.

"Colonel Keays," Jimmy gasped. His voice scratched his throat as he spoke. His eyes darted up and down the colonel's uniform, taking in every detail, as if something Jimmy saw might reveal the man as an impostor, while the real Colonel Keays was down on the ground somewhere, running the CIA.

But it was the same blue uniform, with the same gold trim. His hat was perched neatly on the edge of the seat and his chest was covered in the same rainbow of medals. Jimmy looked closer. Next to a row of multicoloured ribbons was a gold cross, a silver star and then a black S on a silver disc. Synperco.

"You look almost as surprised to see me as I am to see you, Jimmy," Keays growled. His usual smirk was absent. In its place was a sharp stare that could have accused Jimmy of every crime in the world.

"What's..." Jimmy stopped himself. There were too many questions all rushing to come out at once. At the same time, he didn't feel he could ask any of them. His trust had died. "But the double agents..." Jimmy whispered, frantically trying to puzzle out what was going on. The words of the agent with the trout lips danced round his head. *We all work for Synperco.*

"There are no double agents, Jimmy," Keays announced. "There are only my agents. They're all working for me."

"You are Synperco," Jimmy hissed slowly. He was almost too horrified to let the words out of his mouth. "Synperco is you."

"Ha!" Keays' head rocked back with the violence of his laugh. "Not quite. But it is my company. I'm Director of the CIA, but I'm also Synperco's Managing Director and major shareholder. Until this week it was a relatively small family business. But thanks to your little escapade in the North Sea, and a few similar operations around the world, today it's by far the biggest American energy company. In fact, there are only two oil companies that are bigger – one in Russia and one in the Middle East. But I can deal with them once I'm President."

"President?" Jimmy almost choked on the word.

His blood froze in his arteries. For a second, he lost all feeling in his legs.

"To be President of the USA, Jimmy," Keays explained, "you need three things. One: the support of the Secret Service. Two: the approval of the oil industry. Three: enough money to run an election campaign and fix it so you win. I'm on my way to Washington to tell President Grogan he no longer has the first two of these things. Thanks to you, Jimmy, I have all three. Grogan will announce a general election before the end of the week."

He straightened his uniform and added casually,

"How do you think I'll look in front of the White House, Jimmy?"

37 NOBODY'S ASSET

All Jimmy could hear was the thudding of his heart in his chest. He wanted it to beat faster to match his nervous energy, but his programming kept it calm. The result was the steady accumulation of hatred in his veins.

"I travelled 1500 miles across America," he rasped, glaring straight into Keays' eyes, "through eleven states, hiding from the police and fighting for my life, to bring you the information that there were missiles hidden on Neptune's Shadow." Jimmy felt his muscles glowing with heat, ready to explode into action. It took all his concentration to stop himself attacking. "I begged you to send me to destroy those missiles and almost died trying. But there were never any missiles there, were there?"

Keays didn't answer. His face didn't even flicker.

"It was all lies!" Jimmy shouted, bursting with rage. He held his head in his hands as the extent of the deception became clear. "You attacked the plane," he whispered. "My plane out of New York. You made me think NJ7 was shooting us down, but... but..." Jimmy felt the heat inside his body growing and sweat glistening on his skin.

"Was there no other way of doing it?" he asked. "Was I the only one who could have given you Neptune's Shadow?"

"Yes, Jimmy," Keays admitted. "Who else could have infiltrated Neptune's Shadow without it looking like a US operation? And you would never have agreed to do it if I'd just asked, would you?"

Jimmy didn't flinch. He was too horrified to respond.

"You killed him," he spat. "You killed your own agent just to make it look like I had to get back to you. I know Bligh was part of the trick, I saw him alive. But what about Froy? You killed him!" Jimmy's face twisted in horror.

"Ha!" Keays blasted. His face wasn't smiling though. There was just a sparkle in his eye. "You're a smart boy, Jimmy, but it looks like you haven't got everything figured out."

Keays glanced past Jimmy's shoulder. Jimmy spun round, following the colonel's eyes. Ducking through a curtain, with a glass of red wine in each hand, was a tall, broad man with dark blond hair and skin that was so tanned it could have been shoe leather. It was the same man who had been escorting Jimmy away from

New York to safety, the other agent that Jimmy thought he saw being killed on the plane – Agent Froy.

"No," Jimmy gasped. "How did...?"

Froy looked up at Jimmy with a small smile and a shrug. Jimmy twisted back to face Keays.

"But I saw them die!" Jimmy insisted.

Keays looked serious again.

"Not everything is as it looks, Jimmy," he replied impatiently. "You, for example."

There was a long silence. Jimmy scowled, while Keays looked strangely relaxed. Jimmy wondered what he was thinking. *Will he try to kill me?* Jimmy wasn't afraid. He was on alert for anything Keays might try, while all the time he was feeling for any slight change in the vibrations in the carpet, sensing any movement from Froy behind him.

"It's a shame you saw Bligh," Keays said at last, still examining Jimmy carefully, as if he was trying to read his thoughts. "That wasn't meant to happen." He sighed and shook his head. "And if you hadn't, you would be safe somewhere and you'd still trust me."

"But you'd use me again, wouldn't you?" Jimmy asked. "Next time you had something too difficult or dangerous – you'd find a way to trick me into doing it."

Keays' lips curled into a smile.

"Sit down, Jimmy," he said gently. "This doesn't need to end in tears. Come and meet the President with me.

The CIA can still keep you safe. You're a valuable asset."

Jimmy wanted to scream. *I'm nobody's asset*, he vowed in his head. How could he have been so stupid? He stood there, absolutely motionless, while Froy passed Keays a glass of wine, took the seat next to him, and the two men leaned back to enjoy the flight. Jimmy tried to remember every single detail about everything that had happened since his plane had been attacked. What were the signs he should have seen? What slight doubts did his programming notice that would have told him the whole oil rig mission was a fake, but which the human fool brushed aside?

Jimmy could feel his hands trembling. He chose to focus on the pain from his palms to distract himself from his own mistakes. But it was impossible. The torture in his mind was far worse than any physical injury. Because of his mistakes, the British were going to war with France. *It's up to me*, he thought. *I can put this right. I have to.*

Keays raised his glass to Jimmy and grinned.

"To a better world!" he announced.

Jimmy suddenly dropped backwards, landing on his hands. His legs sprung out like cobras' tongues, smashing the two glasses. Red wine and glass splattered all over Froy and the colonel. Before they could even react, Jimmy flipped over his hands and rolled backwards, down the centre of the plane, towards the cockpit.

As soon as he was on the other side of the curtain,

he jumped to his feet and tore open the flimsy door that separated the cabin from the cockpit.

"Your flight's over," said Jimmy firmly, grabbing the pilot by the shoulders. The man was big and struggled in Jimmy's grip, but he had no chance. Jimmy threw him into the cabin. He knew the plane would continue steadily for a few seconds without anybody's hands on the controls.

"Jimmy!" hollered Colonel Keays from the cabin. His voice boomed and seemed to shake the whole plane. "There's nowhere you can go now, Jimmy." His voice was getting closer. "And there's nothing you can do."

He burst into the cockpit. He was holding a pistol. Jimmy was ready for him. He turned to the right and stepped to the left. At the same time he grabbed Keays' wrist and pulled. They were both facing the same direction now, with Jimmy holding Keays' gun hand out in front. Then Jimmy jabbed his elbow into Keays' throat.

The noise Keays made was like a drowning rat. He immediately dropped the gun and staggered backwards, out of the cockpit. His eyes bulged in their sockets. Jimmy followed him, ducking so that Keays' body was a shield, and quickly snatched three parachutes from the wall.

Keays fell back through the curtain, grasping at his throat and wheezing to catch his breath. Jimmy punched a parachute into his midriff. The blow sent air into Keays' lungs and reopened his windpipe.

The pilot and Froy were waiting on either side of the entrance to the cabin, both armed with handguns. Jimmy wanted to dive out of the way, but his programming wouldn't let him. *Move*, he begged his legs, but they wouldn't. Instead, he lingered for a fraction of a second, directly between Froy and the pilot.

It was just long enough to make them both shoot. That's when Jimmy folded to the ground. The bullets hummed over him as he fell, grazing the skin on the top of his head. Then each bullet found a home in the opposite man's knee. As Jimmy had been directly between them, they had accidentally shot each other.

They both collapsed to the floor, clutching their legs in agony and crying out. Jimmy threw a parachute on to each of them, dragged them to the emergency exit and pulled the door's release lever.

"Here you are, Prime Minister," Miss Bennett announced, dropping a block of paper bound with a black plastic spine on to the PM's desk.

"What's this?" mumbled Ian Coates. He was scribbling some notes and didn't move his head, but looked up with his eyes, lingering on the top of Miss Bennett's legs.

"What do you think it is?" Miss Bennett snarled. "Unless there's more than one country you're thinking of going to war with this week?"

The Prime Minister gave a 'harumph' and picked up the dossier. He leaned back in his chair and thumbed through it.

"Anything good in here?" he asked, at last making eye contact.

"The usual," Miss Bennett replied. "There are some economic strategies to weaken France before we strike, which you won't understand, details of how to strike, which you'll enjoy, and the consequences of striking, which you'll ignore. Don't I always give you the best?"

She raised an eyebrow and struck a pose with one hand on her hip and the other toying with a stray hair by her cheek. After a second of silence, Miss Bennett's eye was distracted by something unusual on the Prime Minister's desk. Among the piles of papers was a small, transparent plastic tub, full of creamy yellow cubes about the size of dice. Miss Bennett peered closer at the label, but it wasn't in English.

"What's that?" she asked.

"This?" Ian Coates pulled the lid off the tub and carefully picked out one of the cubes. "It's a gift from the Icelandic Government. They wanted to show us their support in our trouble with France."

"It smells awful," said Miss Bennett, pulling away slightly.

"It's called *Hákarl* apparently. It's putrefied shark meat."

"How does it taste?"

"I haven't tried it yet." The Prime Minister rolled the cube in his fingertips, his hand hovering in front of his mouth. His lips parted. But then suddenly he seemed to change his mind. Instead of eating it, he put his cube of shark meat on the desk and held out the tub to Miss Bennett. "Why don't you try some first?"

38 SOMEONE YOU NEED

When Jimmy pulled the release lever of the emergency exit, the effect was immediate. Since he had boarded the plane, the pilot had increased their altitude considerably. The difference in air pressure between the inside and outside of the cabin was relatively small, but it was more than enough to create massive suction.

Jimmy gripped the edge of the doorway as the door itself swung out. He dug his heels into the carpet. The others had nothing to save them. The pilot was the first to go, then Froy whooshed out half a second later. Despite their injuries, both men had the presence of mind to shove an arm through the straps on their parachutes.

Finally, Colonel Keays slid across the carpet, desperately clawing at the fibres to keep himself inside the plane. His nails etched tracks into the bloody handprints that Jimmy had made on the floor.

When Keays was close enough, Jimmy grabbed his collar, while keeping hold of the door with his other hand.

"You're taking too long to leave," he muttered. Jimmy dragged Keays right up to the threshold, until the man's body was flying out of the door. The colonel had dropped his parachute though, so Jimmy picked it up and put one of the straps over the man's head. He was about to let go, when the colonel reached out and seized Jimmy by the shoulder.

Jimmy was shocked. He stared into the colonel's eyes. They were pale green, like a lizard's, and his eyebrows made two sharp points above them.

"You need me!" Keays yelled. His voice had almost completely disappeared – he still hadn't recovered from Jimmy's blow, but he wasn't giving up. Jimmy could see power in his eyes. He pulled the colonel close, until he could feel the warmth of the man's breath.

"I'll never need anybody," Jimmy snarled, his whole being pulsating with his assassin's wrath.

"I have someone you need," said Keays.

"Go and tell the President, Colonel."

Jimmy relaxed the muscles in his hand, letting go of Keays' collar and shook his shoulder to loosen the colonel's grip on him. Keays dug his fingers in.

"What about Felix's parents?" the man whispered. Then he let go of Jimmy's shoulder.

"What?" Jimmy gasped. He threw himself forwards to catch Keays' collar again. The fabric of the man's uniform brushed through his fingertips. But Jimmy had no grip. There was too much blood covering his hand and not enough skin. He reached out, making one last grab to bring Keays back and question him, but too late.

Colonel Keays hurtled away from him, a twisted smile on his face. Jimmy's head flooded with a million thoughts at once – about Keays, the CIA, NJ7, the Muzbeke family...

"Where are they?" Jimmy screamed into the sky. "What have you done with them?"

His words were blown back into his face. Before his sentence was even finished, his view of Colonel Keays was blocked by the black satin canopy of the parachute.

Jimmy leaned out as far as he could, peering around the wing and trying to make out where Keays would land. It was impossible. Jimmy turned back to the cabin, but he knew only too well that with only three people on the plane there would only be three parachutes. *I could still jump after him*, he heard himself thinking. *I'd find some way to land. I'll track down Keays.* What did the CIA want with Neil and Olivia Muzbeke? Jimmy's mind reeled.

I'll make Keays tell me where they are.

Jimmy knew that was crazy. The shaking of the plane forced him to come to his senses. He hauled the emergency door closed and rushed to the cockpit. When his hands took the controls of the plane, he was acting automatically.

He wasn't even aware of the brutal rumble of the engines. While his programming steadied the flight and took the plane back up to cruising altitude, his mind was a storm of a thousand thoughts.

It felt like everything in the world had stopped being real and become an illusion. Keays had only been protecting him in order to use him. NJ7 hadn't attacked the spy plane, the CIA had. There never had been missiles on Neptune's Shadow.

Jimmy's thoughts didn't stop there. He couldn't control them. He started to believe that nothing in the world had ever been as it seemed. *My father isn't my father*, he heard in his head. *My body looks normal, but it isn't.* He watched the plane's control panel as his hands spread blood-prints all over it. But then the flow of blood slowed. His hands stopped throbbing. He was healing already.

I'm not human, Jimmy thought. *This isn't real.* He repeated it, over and over, as if his own mind was spiralling away from him.

"NO!" he shouted suddenly, as if bursting out of a dream. "NO!" He screamed it until his voice rattled the glass of the cockpit window.

Georgie. His mother. Felix. Their faces flashed through his mind. They were in danger. *When Britain attacks France it won't be an illusion*, he thought. *Or when France retaliates.*

Jimmy glanced at the fuel gauge and checked the wind speed. Then he read off his navigational heading and set about the plane's switches. The Falcon 20 wheeled round, making a sharp left turn. Instead of following America's east coast from New York down towards Washington, Jimmy was speeding out over the Atlantic. He was heading for Europe.

Still the image of Keays' escaping taunted him. When Jimmy tried to shake it off, the man's face morphed into Ian Coates.

If they want a fight, they've got one, he cried in his head. His muscles seemed to growl, ready for action. *No more lies*, he thought. *Except my own.*

Can Jimmy save his family
AND prevent a war?
The choice is simple.
The decision is deadly.

SNEAK PREVIEW...

First it was a light on the dashboard, then a noise in the engine. A tiny 'clunk' that you would only notice if you knew what to listen out for. Jimmy Coates knew what to listen for, and he knew it meant trouble. Running out of fuel is inconvenient if you're driving a car, but if you're ten thousand metres up in the air in a small plane, it's usually fatal.

Jimmy didn't panic. He'd been expecting this for the last three hours. *I could land*, he thought. At that moment he was somewhere over the middle of the Atlantic Ocean, so it would be tricky, but he knew he could do it. Even though the Falcon 20 wasn't designed to go anywhere near water, Jimmy pictured himself splashing down into the waves. A part of his brain was already working out the best angle for the plane to hit the water. He could even feel the muscles in his shoulders warming, preparing for the longest swim of his life.

He gritted his teeth and stared straight ahead out of the cockpit. He knew landing wasn't an option. He had to reach Europe. Thousands of lives could depend on it. Then came the answer.

The plane rocked slightly. A roar drowned out the sound of the Falcon's engines. Jimmy peered upwards, squinting at the brightness of the sky. There it was – the shadow of a commercial jet looming above him.

"Time to catch a lift," Jimmy whispered under his breath. He glanced one more time at the fuel gauges. They were deep in the red zone. *Ignore them*, Jimmy ordered himself. *It's enough. It has to be.* With that, he powered the Falcon higher.

His fingers glided over the plane's controls. Blood covered his palms – black, coagulated blood that left tacky marks on every switch and button. But they were healing already. He could feel it. The pain was far away, buried by his senses. He stared at his hands, but saw past the shredded streaks of red and black skin to the dull grey layer underneath.

Next to the Airbus A490, Jimmy's Falcon plane was like a fly around the back end of a hippopotamus. Jimmy's mouth dropped open at the enormousness of it. He guessed it must have been nearly a hundred metres long, with an even larger wing span. Its deep rumble vibrated in Jimmy's chest.

Sooner than he expected, Jimmy was flying directly beneath it, with only a few metres separating the

Falcon's roof from the undercarriage of the Airbus. *I hope this works,* Jimmy thought. He took a deep breath and lowered his shoulders, searching inside himself for that familiar buzz. He knew it was coming. It had to.

He let the world fall into a blur, focusing all his energy on a point deep inside him, somewhere between his stomach and the base of his spine. He needed that power to take over completely. He knew that's where his plan had come from. Jimmy could never have dreamt up anything so outrageous otherwise.

Then, like an exploding geyser, Jimmy's muscles flooded with energy. His arms felt lighter than air. His neck fizzed and his brain throbbed in his skull. Jimmy was full of hatred and exhilaration at the same time. This would save him, he told himself. But at the same time there was a tiny voice inside that knew this power would also, eventually, destroy him...

Jimmy Coates is a
boy with a secret
and even he doesn't
know what it is.
But it's a matter of
life and death...

HarperCollins *Children's Books*

Jimmy Coates
is on the run.
But how can he
survive when his
enemy's greatest
weapon is a boy
just like him?

HarperCollins *Children's Books*

With his family torn
apart and his life in
danger, Jimmy seeks
refuge in the USA.
But the enemy is
inside his head.

HarperCollins *Children's Books*